THE WEDDING OF MOLLY O'FLAHERTY

SIERRA SIMONE

CHAPTER 1

SILAS

I felt her absence long before I opened my eyes, long before I sat up and began thinking coherent thoughts. I felt her absence in the cool sheet at my side, in the gnawing pit in my chest, in the emptiness in my heart.

I had woken up alone every morning for the past nine months. This morning was no different.

No different at all.

I sat up, dug the heels of my hands in my eyes and tried to ignore the tears burning at the backs of my eyelids.

CASTOR—ALSO known as the Baron or, more formally, as Lord Gravendon—paced by the doorway to the morning room. The smell of breakfast still hung in the air, and the sun had not yet beat away the morning fog. "And she left without a word?"

I stood with my forehead pressed to the cool glass of the window, not bothering to look away from the mist-covered lawn. "She did."

"That's never been her way. The quiet way."

"That's how I know she means it. The leaving. Last night was a farewell for her." I took a deep breath and mustered the courage to utter the next words out loud. "She never intended on staying."

The Baron paused his movements. "Does she know yet? About her fiancé's connection to the board?"

I sighed. "No."

Molly was engaged to Hugh Calvert, a viscount who also happened to be a cousin of the leader of her company's board, Frederick Cunningham. A fact that we were positive she didn't know, and yet were unsure how to bring up. Because effectively, what did it change? She was still forced to marry Hugh, she still had no legal recourse to change that, and she'd made it clear that my interference in her upcoming marriage only brought her pain.

Except.

Except I still planned on interfering. As much as possible.

A footman entered the room with a low bow, a letter resting on a silver salver. "Mr. Cecil-Coke. A message, sir."

The Baron and I exchanged equally confused glances. I walked over to the footman, thanking him for the letter, taking it back to my spot at the window.

I unfolded the letter, skimming quickly through the words as my heart began to pound.

The Baron, perhaps noticing my excitement, stepped forward. "Is it from Molly?"

"Even better," I said, tucking the letter into my pocket and making my way to the door. "It's from my banker."

"Good news?"

"The best. Where's Julian?"

MOLLY

When my fiancé stormed into my house, I was sitting peacefully at breakfast, reading one of the morning papers, blowing on a fresh cup of tea—my broken heart safely hidden and all signs of the night I just shared with Silas sluiced away with hot water and soap.

Hugh came into the dining room looking ready to do battle, with color high in his cheeks and breathing fast, his normally handsome features folded into an expression of pure, indignant rage. But when he saw me sitting there, fresh and serene and very obviously involved in a leisurely breakfast, he paused.

"Good morning, Hugh," I said pleasantly. "Sleep well last night?"

He opened his mouth and then shut it. Clearly he expected something different when he came in here—perhaps for me to be rumpled and freshly fucked or perhaps for me to be absent altogether. But, as always, he'd underestimated my intelligence.

To be fair, I'd underestimated his capacity for ruthless cunning. It shamed me to think of all those years I'd justified Hugh's inclusion into our circle, despite Silas and Julian's obvious distrust of him. I'd found Hugh to be charming and handsome and exactly the kind of lover I felt the most comfortable with—passive and easygoing, with lots of grace in the ballroom and lots of stamina in the bedroom. But since our engagement had become official a few weeks ago, Hugh had become possessive, punitive, avaricious—at least, I assumed it was avarice that drove his latest series of actions, which consisted of contracts and enforced morality clauses

3

that would strip me of my company the moment I was anything less than the perfectly loyal wife.

Many women wouldn't have thought twice about that. *Of course*, wives were expected to be faithful models of decorum, *of course*, no respectable English wife would ever dabble in infidelity. But my friends and I lived by different standards, and a part of me had always assumed that Hugh would accept that the business-like nature of our marriage necessitated leeway along the traditional boundaries. I never considered that someone I counted a friend would reveal himself to be so conservative, so frankly misanthropic about what I'd thought were shared understandings about sensuality and desire.

I'd been mistaken. And now I was about to enter into a loveless marriage without even the personal freedoms I thought every enlightened woman was entitled to. I suppressed the flash of anger I had at this thought; I'd made my decision and I'd also made my goodbye to the one man I'd regret leaving behind. I had no choice in this matter if I wanted to see O'Flaherty Shipping remain alive.

I set down my newspaper, but I didn't rise to my feet to go to him, nor did I invite him to sit. The contract outlined the mechanics of my duties—it said nothing about the attitude with which I carried them out. I could be polite, I could even endure our marriage bed when the time came, but he would get no more from me than that.

Hugh finally spoke, his voice strained when he did, as if he was still trying to accept that his energy and anger had been for nothing. "I heard at the club this morning that someone saw your carriage going back to the Baron's. And I thought…"

I wasn't going to lie. Hugh had tainted my behaviors enough. "I went back to the Baron's last night, but only for a couple hours. And if it's my chastity you're concerned with, don't be. I didn't have intercourse with a man." I hoped the bitterness in my tone covered over the specificity of my words. Because I indeed had refrained from intercourse with a man, but Viola had fucked me with her fingers, right before Silas had come all over my face. Again, I'd been faithful to the letter of my marriage contract, if not to the spirit of it.

As I predicted, Hugh only focused on the bitterness, dropping into the chair across from me, his face pained. And for a moment, I saw the young man I'd befriended several years ago, affable and out of his depth with any matter more serious than a fox hunt.

"I just want our marriage to be a success, Molly." He reached for my hand, and I reluctantly let him take it. "For both our sakes. I want you to be happy, to have everything you want."

That was demonstrably not true, but a small part of me wanted to believe it was. To believe that maybe I still had a chance for happiness—or at the least, the independence to run my company—despite everything that had happened.

"My lawyers and I will be finalizing the contract today," I said, pulling my hand away and changing the subject. "And the preparations for our engagement party this week are nearly complete."

"And our wedding?" he asked eagerly. "The sooner we set a date, darling, the sooner we can move on with our lives."

And the sooner my life will end.

"As we discussed, the end of this month."

"And a honeymoon?" He gave me a look that was unmistakably tender. "I'm ready for us to start a family, Molly. *Our* family."

I stared at him. As astute as I could be at reading people, Hugh still remained a murky figure in my mind. He seemed genuinely earnest to marry me, to possess my body and heart as his and his alone, at the same time that he seemed eager to lay legal claim to my money and my business. I could only conclude that it was a mixture of both things—that he was doing this because he carried some sort of misguided affection for me *and* a very real desire for my holdings.

And then I remembered Silas last night, his impassioned speech on the ballroom floor, the incandescent passion that burned between us in bed, with Viola as our tinder. Heat flared deep in my stomach at the same time pain squeezed my heart.

"Whatever you wish, Hugh," I said, suddenly ready to be by myself. "And if you'll excuse me, I need to prepare for my lawyers. You can expect the contract very soon."

He felt his dismissal and, thankfully, accepted it without argument. He stood and kissed my hand. "I want to see you soon, Molly," he said in a low voice. "Please don't avoid me now—I don't want you to interpret our contract to mean that I want to conduct our engagement entirely within the bounds of propriety…"

He clearly thought he was being charming here, and I felt the kindling of a white-hot anger behind my eyes. *He thinks I'll still fuck him of my own free will? After trapping me with my own company?* No, I wouldn't submit to that humiliation until it was absolutely unavoidable.

Dangerously close to saying something I'd regret, I stood as well, taking my hand back and moving toward the door with him trailing behind me. I resisted the urge to ball my fists or stomp my feet, despite the sudden rage, and instead I cleared my throat and spoke calmly, "Perhaps it's easier if we do things the traditional way. After all, I now need to legally protect myself against aspersions against my character, and I'm worried that premarital liaisons between us may complicate that."

His mouth pressed together in a thin line, the effect of

which made him look ten years older and strangely familiar...

"You can't argue with this," I continued. "This is your own contract, your demands, that you've brought to me. I'm only trying to abide by them."

I saw him struggle with this information, searching for counter-arguments and finding none. After all, he could hardly threaten me for daring to be chaste. At least before our marriage. Afterwards, I would have no choice but to submit, but until then, my body would remain my own.

Hugh gave me a curt bow and donned his hat. "In that case, I will wish you a good day and the best of luck with your lawyers."

I shut the door behind him with a sigh of relief. And then I calmly walked back to the table, where I just as calmly took my teacup off the table and hurled it against the wall.

"EVERYTHING IS MORE or less in order, Miss O'Flaherty," my attorney said. "We only wanted to clarify a few more things before we arranged for your signatures."

We sat in my office, myself and three of my lawyers, piles of onionskin paper stacked between us. I set down the pen I'd just taken up with a sigh. "What is it?" I asked.

They glanced at each other. Aaron Caldwell, my lead attorney, seemed to be the one silently nominated to explain. He looked down at the papers as we spoke, shuffling through a few of them. "We took the liberty of investigating Mr. Calvert's holdings. Which is very standard, of course, in such a union as yours, where both parties are bringing consider-able wealth to the marriage."

I rolled my hand through the air. "Yes, Mr. Caldwell, I know."

Get to your point, I wanted to scream but didn't. This day was awful enough without me alienating the few people left on my side.

"Well, Miss O'Flaherty, the thing is…Mr. Calvert *isn't* bringing considerable wealth to your marriage."

I froze. "Excuse me?"

"The Beaumont viscounty is quite depleted, both in land and in liquid assets, mainly due to some bad investments made by the Viscount's late father. Mr. Calvert is actually in a very threadbare financial state."

"How could that be?" I sputtered. I'd never seen Hugh lacking for money, *ever*, not when we were in Europe and not here in England. He'd always worn the most fashionable clothes and stayed in the most fashionable hotels, and never had he indicated that it was difficult for him to do so.

"Apparently, he has been sustained by loans from a relative." Mr. Caldwell took a breath as the other lawyers shifted in their seats. "And we feel that you should know that the relative is Frederick Cunningham."

It was as if the sound left the room, the sound and all the air and all the light, and for a moment there was nothing but a dull ringing and the knowledge that I'd been duped. Led. Manipulated.

Thoroughly and utterly fooled.

Mr. Caldwell kept talking. "It appears that Mr. Cunningham is a first cousin to Mr. Calvert, on his mother's side. The age difference and Mr. Cunningham's lack of title have meant that the two have never associated openly in the same social circles, but regardless, it's been Mr. Cunningham keeping Mr. Calvert's lifestyle in the manner in which he seems to have been accustomed."

"No wonder Cunningham was so insistent that I marry Hugh," I said, mostly to myself. Hugh had arrived only a couple of weeks before the board had laid down their edict, and at the time, I found his presence a happy coincidence. He kept me company, went to parties with me, played the part of a concerned friend, and now it was all too clear that he'd been courting me, hoping I'd choose him. And when that didn't happen on its own, Cunningham stepped in and forced the choice upon me.

I turned to my lawyers, all of whom I trusted and all of whom had been indispensable through this crisis. "Does this change anything about my position in the company?" I asked bluntly. "Does this mean I can avoid marrying?"

"There is a clear conflict of interest here, but again, since the board would be acting purely of their own free will if they sold their shares—something they all have the freedom to do if they choose—there's nothing legally reproachable here. Ethically, yes. But in a court of law...we would not be able to make a case."

I stared down at my hands. "So the fact that this marriage directly benefits a member of the board is inconsequential?"

Their silence was sufficient.

I picked up my pen and unstoppered my inkwell. "Then I suppose I'm just as trapped as before."

"With all due respect," Mr. Caldwell said, "you still have the choice not to marry."

"And lose my company?"

"In a legal sense, you are already losing it." Mr. Caldwell placed a large hand over the contract, preventing me from sliding it over to my side of the desk. "Please, Miss O'Flaherty. I'm saying this as an acquaintance who has the greatest respect and affection for you. There is so little to be gained from this match—there is a very real chance that you will be separated from your company and will not have any recourse anyway. Would it be so unthinkable to let the board sell their shares?"

"It would ruin the company," I said flatly, pulling at the contract.

He let go, but his voice and posture remained impassioned. "And what then? With your land investments and other assets, we could make sure that you were comfortable the rest of your days, and then you would be free to marry whom you wanted."

"I appreciate your concern, Mr. Caldwell," I said, irritated. Not irritated with him or his well-meant advice, but with everything else. This situation. This business climate. This country. "But this company is *mine*. My father and I built it from nothing after we lost everything, and I will do whatever I have to do in order to keep it alive. Understood?"

I signed the contract, my signature dark and spiky on the paper.

A knock at the door prevented the lawyers from answering. I rubbed my forehead. It was barely noon, and between Hugh and the contract, I was feeling quite done with the day. An unexpected visitor did not bode well.

My butler came to the office door. "A Miss van der Sant, madam."

My eyebrows raised. Birgit van der Sant was the adolescent daughter of Martjin van der Sant, a man that O'Flaherty Shipping was in negotiations to partner with for business. She'd also caught the eye of the predatory Frederick Cunningham, who had a known proclivity for young women.

Known by me, at least.

I shivered and pushed away the dark memories.

"Let her in, Mason," I told my butler. "Show her into the parlor, and I'll be in shortly."

CHAPTER 2

MOLLY

*B*irgit sat on my sofa, her gloved hands twisting in her lap. When I entered the parlor, she looked up, her young face caught in an expression of vulnerable hope... which vanished after a few seconds, replaced by a calm facade of impassivity. I thought of her father—a stern older man with a reputation for rigid Teutonic morality—and decided she probably often had to hide her most vulnerable feelings, her most tumultuous ones. Martjin van der Sant did not seem like the kind of father who would indulge in displays of emotion.

She stood as I walked to her, and we clasped hands and exchanged kisses.

"Miss van der Sant," I said, sitting and indicating she should do the same. "I'm quite pleased to see you, although I confess I'm a little surprised. How can I help you today?"

She sucked her lower lip into her mouth for an instant before releasing it, a childhood habit superseded by conscious control of her mannerisms, girlhood being subsumed by adulthood. For some reason, that made my heart squeeze, in nostalgia and regret all at the same time.

"You remember, the day before last, when you said to tell you if Mr. Cunningham asked to speak with me alone?"

My chest squeezed again, with anger this time. I kept my voice even as I answered. "Yes, I remember."

"Yesterday evening he invited Father and me over for supper at his house. We went…and after the meal, when the ladies were retiring to the parlor, he caught me in the hallway."

I tamped down the urge to fly out of my seat and start throwing things, but the strain showed in my voice when I asked, "Did he touch you?"

She shook her head vehemently. "No, Miss O'Flaherty. I kept myself a respectable distance away from him at all times."

"I hate that you feel it's your job to maintain that respectful distance," I said. "Please continue."

She looked down at her gloves, her cheeks blushing a vulnerable shade of red. Shame colored her words when she spoke again. "He said that he enjoyed my company very much and wanted to see more of me while I stayed here in London. I said something about how Father and I would be happy to accept any invitations he might offer, but then he interrupted and said, 'I think you understand that I am not talking about your father.'

"I felt sick with his words, because I knew then that you had been right. I made my excuses and left, and then I found Father and told him I was ill and that I needed to return to the hotel." She took a deep breath, and I breathed my own quiet sigh of relief. She'd kept her wits about her and escaped unscathed. Thank God.

I put my hand over hers. "You did the right thing, Miss

van der Sant. And you also did the right thing coming to me. I'll make sure Cunningham can't bother you again."

"Excuse me, Miss O'Flaherty, but I'm not finished," Birgit said in a soft voice. "Because he found me this morning. Father had meetings early, and so I took breakfast with my hired chaperone in the hotel dining room. She saw acquaintances across the room and went over to say hello...and once she did, Mr. Cunningham sat down at my table." Her chin trembled. "He said he'd been waiting for me."

I peered into her soft gray eyes, mosaics of fear and shame and the hidden iron kernel of strength every teenage girl carries with her. "What did he say to you, Birgit?"

The use of her Christian name seemed to comfort her a little. "He said that he wanted...*me*." The shakiness with which she pronounced *me* made it very clear that she understood Cunningham's meaning. "And he said that he was going to have me. And that if I tried to stop him, he would tell my father I'd been behaving loosely in London with several young men, and he would see to it that not only would I lose Father's love, but that I would lose any chance of making a good match." She swallowed.

"Mother Mary," I whispered. I had thought there was no level of depravity that Cunningham could sink to that would surprise me...but here I was, surprised. I shouldn't have been —with both Birgit and me, he had used our love of our fathers as leverage.

"He named a time and a place. I—" She broke off, fumbling in her small lace bag, fishing out a card with an address scrawled on the back. I recognized that address: The Hedgehog, his gentlemen's club. I took the card and studied it, and then she admitted in a quiet voice. "I managed to escape my chaperone and come here to you."

"It's going to be okay," I assured her. "We will make sure that you stay safe."

A shine of tears in her eyes. "But I couldn't help it. I agreed to meet him."

"Oh, Birgit," I said.

"How can I say *no*, Miss O'Flaherty, when if I don't do as he asks, he will tell all those terrible lies to Father?"

Even though I already suspected the answer, I had to be sure. "And would your father believe him? Over your own word and what he knows to be true of your character?"

"Father is a good man," she said slowly. "And he loves me. But like many good men, he is quick to believe the worst about others."

We sat for a few moments without speaking, her words lingering in the air as I turned the card over in my fingers, the card stock scratching gently at my skin. I wanted to tell Birgit that she must not go, under any circumstances. That whatever else she had to endure, however hard it was to prove her innocence to her father, that everything would be so much better if she refused Mr. Cunningham outright. That even if she didn't have the belief and trust of those around her, she could still cling to the certainty that she'd done nothing wrong. Because that was the genius of Cunningham's manipulations—he made you feel complicit in his depravity. It didn't matter how cerebrally and intellectually I knew that I had been just a girl, that I had been innocent, that the way he'd forced my body to respond did not negate the horror of what he'd done. Because as soon as I would repeat those thoughts to myself, as soon as I would comfort myself with the knowledge that he was the monster and that nothing I'd done made him any less so, then I would move on with my day and my thoughts would gradually drift to other matters, and soon enough, those ugly whispers in my mind would resurface again. It was an un-winnable battle.

I wanted to spare Birgit that.

But I couldn't ignore the very real threat Cunningham had laid before her. His actions would have real consequences, consequences that could ruin Birgit's life. And even if, miraculously, her Puritanical father believed her over the word of another businessman, Cunningham could still undermine her chances for a good marriage.

"We must tell your father about this plot, you and me together," I said. "Before anything else transpires. We have Cunningham's card, and I will tell your father my own story. That should be enough to cast doubt on his character."

Birgit was already shaking her head. "He will dismiss it as a story. My father *is* a good man, Miss O'Flaherty, but when it comes to matters of the carnal…" She paused and blushed at the word *carnal*. There was no way I was allowing her to endure Cunningham's touch. It had nearly broken me—as sensual and sturdy as my soul was. It would shred this delicate flower. She forced herself onward. "When it comes to those matters, Father can be quite…traditional. He feels that women are the weaker sex on many levels, especially when it comes to things like lying. And he abhors deceit."

"So he would not consider this sufficient proof of wrongdoing on Cunningham's part?" I held up the card. "He would assume you were lying simply because you are female and because he cannot imagine a fellow businessman capable of such horror?"

She nodded. "He couldn't imagine it…unless there was strong proof."

I handed her the card back, things finally fitting together for me. There was a reason I had run O'Flaherty Shipping successfully for this many years. I was talented at thinking outside the box, and I wasn't afraid to be ruthless. "Then we force your father to confront the strongest proof we can offer."

"But…" Her gray eyes swept up to mine, searching. "Even

if we were somehow able to contrive such proof, Cunningham's behavior would enrage Father. And even if you were involved in bringing the truth to light, he would still associate the moral taint with you. He would refuse to negotiate with your business any further. You can't make such a sacrifice, not when it involves your company."

I had been about to speak, but I stopped before the words came out. I had not thought of that particular consequence, and it was a serious one. O'Flaherty Shipping needed van der Sant and his ships, much more than he needed us. Without this partnership, we would encounter a shrinking customer base and an ever faster-shrinking profit margin.

But perhaps O'Flaherty Shipping could manage. My father and I had run this business the way we felt was fair and just—with decent wages and honest practices, and I would not sabotage that principle now, especially not when an innocent girl was at risk. And there was the not-insignificant fact that I would be doing incredible injury to Cunningham's reputation. That was perhaps enough salve to soothe whatever loss my company took as a result.

I put a hand on Birgit's shoulder. "If it protects you from that man, then it is truly no sacrifice. Give me this afternoon to plan and consult with some allies, and by tonight, we will have this figured out."

For the first time since our interview had started, she dared a smile. It was small and tremulous and hesitant, but it was definitely a smile. "Do you really think so?"

I squeezed her shoulder as hundreds of possible scenarios ran through my mind—scenarios that ended with Cunningham shamed or even arrested, scenarios that ended with my company faltering despite all I had done to save it. But one look at the frail blond sitting beside me confirmed what I knew deep inside—there was only one decision I could make, as a woman who finally had enough power to protect other women.

"Yes, Birgit. I'm going to help you. You'll see."

SILAS

"We should have done this a decade ago," Julian said, tossing his pen onto the table. I set my own pen down, flexing my cramped hand. We'd been signing papers for what felt like hours, long enough that George was now asleep on a blanket on the floor while Ivy sprawled nearby reading a book.

"I disagree," I said, reaching for a glass of water and wishing it were gin. "I think Molly would have murdered us for interfering with her company."

"You're probably right," Julian conceded. His green eyes swept over the table with their seemingly endless stacks of paper. "Do you think—is it enough, I mean? And are we in time to make a difference?"

"I think anything before she's actually married is in time," I replied with a tired smile. "But will it be enough? I don't know. Honestly, it depends on what she believes."

"I hope she believes it's enough," Julian said. "For her sake, and for the sake of my new holdings in O'Flaherty Shipping."

Me too, I added silently. Out loud, I said, "Thank you, Jules. I wouldn't have been able to do this if it weren't for you."

He shrugged. "I've got more money than I know what to do with. I would have bought shares in Molly's company in a heartbeat if I'd known what kind of danger she was in. I'm just glad you found enough people willing to part with their own shares."

It had been tricky. About a month ago, after I'd come to

London and grasped exactly how precarious Molly's situation was, I'd visited my solicitors and set into motion a plan to quietly buy as many shares of O'Flaherty Shipping as possible. Of course, it would look suspicious if one person was snatching up any and all shares that shareholders were willing to sell, so Julian had agreed to help me. Together, we'd managed to carve out almost twenty percent of the shares—which, added with Molly's shares, gave the three of us forty percent of the company. Not enough to dictate decisions, but maybe enough for the company to survive if the other members of the board made good on their threat to leave.

And then Julian and I had decided not to stop there. Using our old European connections, we discovered a Dutch shipping company that was looking for significant investors to grow its global fleet, and consequently, with a hefty sum and a few signatures, Julian and I were now among the chief shareholders in Van Der Sant Shipping, and we could gift those shares to Molly at any point.

Now, Molly's former board members would no longer be able to weight the scales quite so much in their favor; between Molly, Julian and me, we now had millions of pounds secured in the business, a metaphorical safety net for Molly should her company crumble and fall.

I still hoped it wouldn't come to that.

I still hoped she would marry me.

I set down my glass and then stretched myself along the floor next to George, curling my body around his chubby snoozing one, tracing one of his out-flung arms with my hand.

Julian watched me with amusement. "Do you miss Thomas's children?"

I nodded, not looking away from George. He was such a perfect little replica of his parents, with Ivy's dark hair and already showing signs of Julian's distinctive eyes and mouth. Would Molly and I have a child that was so obviously ours? With red hair and blue eyes and my grin and her freckles?

The thought was too painful to entertain for long.

"After Charlotte has the baby, they're thinking of coming home to Coke Manor for a while," I said, trying to cheer myself up. I loved my nieces and nephews dearly, and I'd always been close to my brother Thomas and his wife. Thomas and I had grown up with parents who loved us and loved each other and who'd made sure to remind us of those things frequently. So now, as an adult, I naturally craved the happy vitality of family life. When I was a younger man, I'd made something akin to a family in Europe with Julian and Molly and the Baron, but nothing could replace the connection I felt with my blood relatives. The longing I felt to be with them again.

That longing was especially strong, given that I would still be alone and unmarried when I rejoined them.

"How long until our work here is official?" Julian asked, changing the subject back to our new investments.

"I believe our signatures were the last ones required. My solicitor told me I should have confirmation of receipt of shares in two days."

"We should wait to tell her," Julian said. "Until things are completely final."

I opened my mouth to argue. I'd wanted to tell her tonight. I'd wanted to whisper it into her ear as we made love with Hugh's blasted contract burning merrily in a fireplace next to us. But I couldn't dispute Julian's suggestion, because of the damage that could be done to Molly's fragile sense of hope if the deal fell through somehow.

Besides, it was only two days, right?

"Yes," I agreed finally. "We will keep it a secret from her until we have confirmation."

I didn't mention that Molly's engagement party was also in two days. It wasn't her wedding, so in a practical sense, it was no impediment to my plan. But in an emotional sense, I couldn't bear the idea of her in front of London, celebrating her upcoming nuptials to another man. Couldn't bear the idea of Hugh clinging to her, of them dancing, of them standing at the door and accepting the effusive congratulations of fashionable acquaintances and near-strangers.

Molly belonged to *me*. The only thing remaining was to prove it.

CHAPTER 3

MOLLY

*T*he Hedgehog hadn't changed in the twelve years since I'd been here. There was the great room, fronted by tall windows and studded with one massive fireplace. There was the dining room with its leather chairs and small tables and globed lamps.

And then there were the rooms upstairs.

Large beds. Maroon curtains. Warm fires.

White sheets. Scarlet sins.

Mr. Cunningham did not always use his favorite club for his assignations, but he used it frequently enough that he had a room of his own set aside. I walked through it now, the manager of the club trailing quietly behind me. He was not happy about any of this—the knowledge of what Mr. Cunningham planned to do or my plan to stop it. But he owed something to the Baron somehow—a debt or a favor—and so he had not actively resisted my decisions about his club tonight.

"Does he bring girls back here often?" I asked, placing my hand on the silk coverlet of the bed. I'd meant to run my hands along the silk casually, possessively, as if to reassure myself that I wasn't scared of this club and I wasn't scared of the place Cunningham slept. But my hand froze the moment it touched the silk, a hundred terrible memories burning through my chest, memories of blood and pain and the feeling of Mr. Cunningham's weight pressing me into the mattress...

The manager stood close to the door, and if my face betrayed any terror or hopelessness or anger, he politely ignored it. "He often...entertains here," the manager said in response to my earlier question. "But nothing like you have described to me. They always appear to be at least one and twenty, or more."

I believed it. This afternoon, I'd called on the Baron, laying the problem of Birgit before him to ask his advice. And then he'd confessed to me that he was no stranger to Cunningham's proclivities, and how, as a result of the Baron's intervention, Cunningham now had to frequent brothels across the Channel to indulge in the services he liked best. So it didn't surprise me that he stayed discreet here in England.

But if he normally kept to less deviant expressions of his desires, then why this pursuit of Birgit? Why now?

Was it some sort of reverse trap? I'd considered that several times today, but I couldn't see how he would risk revealing such a seamy part of his character and still hope to withdraw from the trap with his reputation unscathed. No, he was exposing himself with the belief that he was doing so safely, something that revealed how comfortable and complacent he'd grown.

How soft.

I thanked the manager for his time and paid him the

promised amount for his silence and for his unusual accommodations tonight. I would undoubtedly be bringing his club undue attention and scandal, and for that I felt bad, but the Baron and I had agreed that this was the only way. This was the clearest path forward; it would be painful and perhaps shameful at points, but in the end, Birgit would be safe and Mr. van der Sant would be convinced both of her virtue and of Cunningham's depravity.

In fact, the Baron would be here tonight to help me from backstage, as it were, to oversee that the club and all of the players moved according to our design. He told me that he'd long felt responsible for Cunningham and saw tonight as a chance to atone, and frankly I welcomed the help. It felt nice not to be alone.

And, since the Baron had also confessed that he'd known about the connection between Hugh and Cunningham for years, I had the feeling the Baron was eager to make things up to me, which was a kind intention, even if it was unnecessary. His silence on the knowledge wouldn't have changed things one way or the other, but I understood and appreciated the impulse to atone.

I went downstairs to the dining room, looking for the Baron and ignoring the stares of the gentlemen lounging insouciantly around their tables. The blue-gray haze of cigar smoke couldn't disguise how very female I was, and typically only one sort of female frequented the interior of such establishments. And even then, she was expected to stay within the private boundaries of the club—the upstairs with its bedrooms and implications of sin. She was not welcome in the dining room.

I wasn't welcome in the dining room.

I honestly didn't care how welcome I was, but I didn't see the Baron's massive shoulders or dark hair, and so I decided to go out to the foyer and out the front door, pushing past the irritated footman, who clearly also resented my presence (and my refusal to use the kitchen door in back.)

"This is no place for a lady," said a soft voice behind me.

I spun around, anger hot in my mouth, and then stopped.

And stepped back.

Silas stood in front of me, his blue eyes twinkling, his roguish grin hooked up to one side. Despite the rainy afternoon, he'd stepped out without an overcoat and he was already in evening clothes, a perfectly fitting black coat and pants with white gloves and a tall black hat, which he doffed now as he bowed to me.

I just stared.

"What is it, Mary Margaret? Is it so strange to see a gentleman at a gentleman's club?"

"This isn't your club," I sputtered. "And besides, you are—"

"I'm no gentleman, yes, yes, I know. But what about Julian and Castor? Are you ready to hurl such insults at them?"

And sure enough, Julian and Castor were rounding the corner now, Castor striding forward confidently while Julian adjusted his gloves. Even though I'd seen Castor earlier today and Julian yesterday, the sight of my three closest friends in the world made my throat squeeze tight and my eyelids burn hot and wet with unexpected tears.

They must have sensed this, because a moment later, I was in a cage of strong arms and chests. And I didn't care about how improper it must look for the four of us to be embracing in the middle of the street...in broad daylight much less. I only cared about how, in that moment, I knew that people loved me and cared about me. I knew that no matter how I felt, I was never truly alone.

"We're here. And we're going to help," someone said in my ear. Silas. I remembered other things he'd whispered in my ear, things he'd whispered just last night, and I shivered.

That's my good Molly.

"You're here for me?" I asked, my face still pressed into someone's coat. Julian's maybe.

"Of course," Julian said in his graveled voice. "Castor told us about what that wretched man was planning to do, and knowing that he was also the one making you miserable with your company's future…well, we are all grateful for the chance to put an end to him."

I pulled back and gazed at them, and I was so glad they were here, and I was also so grateful that they'd come here as they did, to support me without a trace of pity or pride. They weren't acting as if I were a damsel in distress—because truthfully, today wasn't about me. It was about Birgit.

A fact which was underscored by Julian muttering something about stopping Cunningham before he could hurt another girl, and the way he said it—and the way the other men reacted—made it painfully clear to me that they didn't know about my own history with Cunningham. There was no awkwardness, no shuffling feet or dodged gazes. I'd hidden my secret well.

Too well.

Suddenly, I was bursting with the need to tell them, to unload the burden I'd carried since I was sixteen. I wanted them to know exactly *how* terrible he was, *how* hurtful, but when I opened my mouth and looked up to their warm, compassionate faces, I couldn't. I couldn't say the words.

"We are meeting Mr. van der Sant for dinner," Julian said, oblivious to my aborted attempt at confession. "And that's when we will bring him upstairs. The girl knows what she needs to say?"

I nodded. "Yes, we've spoken. She knows what to do."

Silas was staring hard at me, and I realized that while Castor and Julian hadn't noticed my small hesitation after the hug, Silas had. I flushed, both with shame and the pressure of his gaze, which was hot and heavy and stirring.

Stop it, I chastised myself. *You left him alone this morning. You were the one who walked away. You can't have him now.*

But I wanted him. I always forgot how powerfully his presence affected me, his tall frame and his lean body and his dimpled grin. I forgot how much my body could remember, how it could feel every kiss and every caress...

I ground my teeth together and willed my desire under control.

"We should go," the Baron said, consulting his pocket watch. "Molly, we will see you in a couple hours."

"You gentlemen go in," Silas said. "I'm going to make sure Molly gets up to her room without any issue."

Julian and Castor made their goodbyes and then trotted up the steps to the front door of the club, disappearing into its gloomy depths. Silas turned back to me, his cerulean eyes appraising.

"We should go in the back," he said quietly, and I agreed. He knew that we couldn't be seen intimately together, not by influential club members and certainly not in Cunningham's own club. Not while my contract with his cousin Hugh was still in place.

I let Silas guide me, trying to control my breathing as his hand firmly grasped my elbow—a gesture that reminded me of the way he'd touched me last night, of his hand wrapped around my jaw as he had ejaculated on my face. I followed him as meekly as a lamb. As I never followed anyone, ever. Not even my own father, who'd dragged me to Liverpool kicking and screaming the entire way.

This was what Silas did to me now. He melted me, molded me, and it made me happier and more content than I'd ever been.

But what did that say about me? Was I not truly the fierce

and independent warrior I'd always imagined myself to be? Was I something more domesticated? Something weaker?

It doesn't matter, I reminded myself. *You will never be with him again.*

Except the way he led me now, so assertively around the back of the building and through the kitchen entrance, as if he were leading me to a *bed* and not just a bedroom...well, my cunt responded exactly as my head couldn't. With undisguised want. With complete and utter acceptance and surrender.

Maybe Silas could sense this, because he didn't let go of me as we walked into the room that the Baron had arranged for us tonight. Instead he closed the door and backed me against the wall, slowly, like a predator cornering its prey.

And then his hands were on either side of me, caging me in, trapping me. My chin tilted up, not in defiance, but in a primally submissive move to expose my throat. He let out a long hissing breath. "You left me," he accused.

"You knew I would," I whispered.

His expression shifted into something harder. "Yes. I did know. That didn't make it any easier to wake up to an empty bed."

"Silas, I can't—"

"Goddammit, Molly!" His hands slammed against the wall next to me, making me jump. But it wasn't anger coursing through him, it was frustration, and I felt that same frustration, I felt it *so much*.

"It can't be any other way."

He leaned in, his blue eyes searching mine. "Not even if tonight takes care of Cunningham?"

I blinked. "Is that why you're here? Because you thought this would end his power over the board?"

"Yes," Silas said bluntly. "And because you needed to lure

van der Sant here, and Julian and I were the best way to do that."

I didn't understand. "Why?"

Silas took a breath, as if wrestling with whether or not he wanted to explain something to me.

This hesitation stoked a fire in me. "Hurry the fuck up, Silas."

This goaded him as I knew it would, and his eyes flashed. "Because, as of today, Julian and I are shareholders in van der Sant's company."

There was a kind of white noise in my mind as I tried to process this, a noise like wind and water and wheels on a smooth road. "You invested in his company?"

Silas nodded.

"But...how? Why?"

And now Silas stepped back, the authority and anger gone, replaced by something gentler, more urbane. He was retreating into his shell, a shell of charm and smiles that had kept him safe for years. "It's a long story," he hedged, taking off his hat and running the brim through his fingers.

"Is it a long story that has something to do with me?" I asked, and even I could hear how dangerous my voice had gotten.

He hesitated.

"Silas," I said in a low voice. "Be honest with me."

"I'd never be anything but honest with you," he said. "But I can't tell you the truth right now."

"So I'm right," I said flatly. "Because it can't be coincidence that you and Julian have decided to do business with the one company that is about to partner with mine."

"We want to help," Silas pleaded, stepping toward me again, but I dodged him.

"Don't you see how terrible that is?" I said, crimson anger filling me, swirling against the inside of my mind like wine in a glass. "Every time somebody tries to help, I start to have hope. And every time that hope is crushed, it's just a little bit worse. It's just a little bit harder. And I can't take it any more —the hope or the failure. I can only handle the certainty, no matter how grim it is."

Silas stopped, his eyes closing for a moment. "That was exactly what Julian and I wanted to avoid." He opened his eyes, and I saw that battle again in their depths, that struggle. There was something more he wasn't telling me.

The crimson anger turned black.

"I am *so sick* of being treated like I can't handle anything!" I cried.

Silas, understandably, looked at a loss. "But you just said you couldn't handle—"

"Never mind what I said! Here's what I want: I want you to treat me as you've always treated me—as an equal. And I want you to leave me alone. Stop interfering and stop trying to rescue me. I don't need either one."

"This is not about us trying to rescue you. Jesus *fuck*, Molly, stop being so goddamned combative for one minute." Silas paced over to the mantle and back again, his long strides eating up the space in the room. He was so leonine, so *masculine* and animal all at once—loping and tall and power-ful. I bit my lip against the sudden drop in my stomach as he turned and I could see the outline of his semi-hard cock against his trousers. Arguing with me was arousing him, and God, that thought would be enough to warm at least a thou-sand of the innumerable cold nights that awaited me after my wedding.

To hide my discomfiture, I lowered myself into the yellow velvet chair by the window. Outside, London settled into an early autumn evening, cool and cloudy, the street already clogged with hansom cabs and horses.

"We're trying to help because you are our friend. Because

we care about you. I know your pride refuses to hear this, but at some point in your life, you will have to accept help when it is freely offered. Help that comes unattached to any sort of economic or emotional exchange, help that just *is*."

"That's called charity," I told him sourly.

"And so what if it is? Are you so willing to hold on to this principle of independence that you won't even consider something that could be beneficial to you and this company you care so much about? Is your pride worth that much?"

That wounded my pride—being called prideful. "I've sacrificed *everything* for this company," I said. "Including my pride. Including my dignity and my self-worth—"

I broke off without meaning to, my throat suddenly too tight to speak, shame crawling over my skin like a swarm of insects.

He was over to me in an instant, dropping to his knees in front of me, his hat tumbling to the floor as he reached for me. His hands found mine, and I didn't resist as he laced our fingers together. He still wore his gloves, and I looked down to study the contrast of my freckled wrists against the white leather.

"Tell me," Silas said, ducking his head so I had to meet his eyes. They burned blue in the dim light, and I never wanted to look away. Except there was still the shame that prickled and skittered over my skin...

"I saw it in your face outside," he continued, his voice soft. "There's something you haven't told us—haven't told me."

"I haven't told anyone," I said. That was a truth which was easier to force out. The truth about the truth. "Except Birgit."

I saw the moment understanding kindled in his eyes. The moment he absorbed the only reason I would tell Birgit my secret when I hadn't told anyone else. The moment that his concern fused together with incandescent rage.

"When." His affect was downward, making it not a question at all, making it an edict instead. I *would* tell him, that tone of voice said, and I would tell him *now*.

And somehow, his change of demeanor unstuck my throat. I couldn't tell my grinning, happy Silas, but I could tell this stern, powerful man who'd spanked me, who'd fingered me in a ballroom, who'd come all over my face while growling harsh, depraved things to me. And somehow, the very idea that this domineering, almost cruel, version of Silas might think less of me because of what I'd done with Cunningham was ridiculous. I don't know why I felt that way, just that something about the way he looked at me now —like he could see beyond my flesh and bone to the soul buried deeply within—told me that he saw me as something untainted and lovely. Something that was his.

"When I was sixteen," I answered after a minute. "Not long after my sixteenth birthday."

"Did he…" Silas's jaw worked as he attempted to restrain his anger. "…Did he *force* you?"

I shook my head, my eyes hot with tears as I started from the beginning of the story. Not with tears of shame, but with tears of relief. I was finally, *finally* telling him about the burden I'd carried for more than a decade. And as I told him, he held himself completely still, completely controlled, even though I could feel the tremor in his hands as he clutched mine harder and harder. As if to reassure himself—and me— that we were here together and I was safe and the things I was describing to him now were securely in the past.

After I finished, Silas took a minute. "I'll kill him," he said eventually, and the words were completely cold and completely calm.

I shivered.

"You can't," I said. "Can't you see that I've thought endlessly about this? There's no way to punish him for what he did. What he still does to me. He's too powerful and my own reputation is too...murky...for me to be a reliable witness. All we can do is protect Birgit." I took a deep breath and said out loud that darkest thought that haunted me. "It's too late for me. He's won. He's defeated me, and he's ruined me. I can't purify myself, I can't fix what he's sullied. I'm tainted now."

Silas pressed his lips together, the deep frown forbiddingly handsome on his face. "No," he said. "I won't hear any more words like that from you." And then he tugged off a glove with his teeth, exposing his bare hand, which now slipped under my skirts.

"Silas," I breathed, still unsteady from my confession. "We can't..."

"I can't touch you with intent to bring pleasure," he interrupted. "This is not a touch to bring about pleasure. This is to remind you whom you belong to. Feel free to use your safe word."

I should. I should use it because we couldn't do this, but then his hand skated over my knee, following my stocking until it ended at the middle of my thigh. And then his fingers were brushing the sensitive skin of my inner thigh, sliding up and toward my center...

My legs fell open of their own accord. Even though I knew I shouldn't allow this, even though I knew Julian or the Baron or—God forbid—Martjin van der Sant could walk into this room at any moment...

"Whom do you belong to, Mary Margaret?" Silas asked.

Now his fingers were *there*, right there, the rough pads seeking out my entrance, and then he shoved two of them harshly inside. He was right, it wasn't about pleasure, it was about possession, except the very nature of such a possessive act was inducing something very, very close to pleasure inside me. My legs widened as far as my skirt would allow, and I was now at the very edge of the chair, shamelessly rocking against his hand.

God. Silas like this. His flesh, his fingers, his fury, as he jabbed his fingers in and out. It hurt so good, my toes curling from the sharp discomfort twined with intense pleasure.

"I said, *whom do you belong to?*" His voice was hoarse now, and I knew without looking that he was hard.

Just that thought made my mouth water. "You," I confessed. "I belong to you."

"Precisely so, Mary Margaret. And *my Molly* doesn't get to talk about herself like that. *My Molly* knows that she's not tainted, she knows that only that monster is to blame. *My Molly* knows that she belongs wholly and entirely to my love and that she's worthy of every single second of it, and not despite of what happened. Because it's part of your history and part of you, and I love every single part of you, wounded or otherwise. *My Molly* knows that she's actually *her own Molly*, that she belongs to herself, that she has never been ruined, because she is still here today, fighting and speaking and feeling."

He'd lied, because now his thumb was rubbing hard against my clit, and he was going to make me come, even though it was forbidden and wrong and dangerous, he was still going to make me come.

"I want you to feel it all right now. All the shame and all the fear and all the hate, and I want you to let it all go. Give it to me, give yourself to me, and I will carry it all for you. For the rest of eternity or even just for a few minutes. Give it to me."

Fire licked everywhere, at the soles of my feet and the insides of my palms and up my neck, but most of all at my core, which burned and flamed at his rough, demanding touch. He shifted, so that he had one foot planted on the floor, while the other knee stayed planted where it was, and his new stance exposed exactly how hard he was, how ready, and I could even see the wet spot on his trousers where he'd started leaking precum. I wished he would say *fuck the contract* and pull his cock out and shove it inside me. I wished he would throw me down and rut into me, press my face into the floor and fuck me until I forgot everything but him, him and his gigantic, perfect dick.

He angled his fingers so that he was rubbing against that one spot inside, and I couldn't take it anymore. My nipples tightened and my belly tightened and my cunt tightened—all of my senses and sensations shrinking to the one point where his touch met my body.

"Oh God," I moaned, my head falling back. "I'm going to... Oh God, Silas..."

"Yes," he groaned. "Let me have it. Let me feel it."

And there it was, all of it, the shame and the fear and the shredded sense of self-worth. It hovered in me as my orgasm hovered just out of reach, and then my orgasm crashed into me, fusing everything into white-hot waves of release. It ripped through my body, out of me and back into me, sending me soaring and falling at the same time; my only tether to reality was Silas's other hand still gripping mine, squeezing hard as I clenched and pulsed around his fingers and rode his hand chasing after every single flutter.

And when I opened my eyes to see Silas staring at me with his face so serious, so stern—eyes hungry and still a little angry—more shudders rippled through me.

He was right. I belonged to him.

He still clasped my hand as he slid his fingers out of me and raised them to his mouth, where he slowly sucked my taste off of each and every one, our gaze never breaking as he did.

I took a deep breath in and a deep breath out, and where I expected shame or regret for violating the contract, I found none. And I found that—just a little, just an infinitesimal amount—my other shame had lessened. It was still there, and I wasn't young or foolish enough to believe it could be wiped out with a single act or a single intention, but it was better.

Lesser.

He was right; he had carried my burden, and carried a part of it still, because he had looked the horrible truth of it in the face and still chosen to love me. As if it didn't matter what I had let Cunningham do to my body or to my mind, because he saw that Molly O'Flaherty was so much more beyond those events, that those events could matter as much or as little as I wanted them to, and that, either way, he would shoulder the load with me while I figured it out.

We sat in silence for just a minute more, my body languidly unwinding and his face no less intense, but before I could speak to thank him, to explain what a gift he'd just given me, he wiped his hand on his pants and then glanced to the clock on the mantel. And like that, the authoritative Silas was gone and my friendly Silas was back in his place, polite smile and all.

"I should go," he said ruefully, getting to his feet and giving my hand one final squeeze.

"Silas…" I stood too, trying to find the words. "I—I want to say *thank you* but that isn't quite right. But I don't know what *is* quite right." I stopped when I noticed the formidable erection still tenting the front of his pants. "Silas, you can't go downstairs like that."

"I'll walk it off," he said with a faux-cheeriness that vanished the moment I stepped forward and pressed my palm against his rigid length, curling my fingers around it through his trousers. A low hiss escaped his lips, and for a minute, I thought maybe he would finish what he'd started. That maybe my commanding Silas would return and order me to the bed, where he'd satisfy us both.

But it wasn't meant to be. He moved backwards, wincing as my hand left his cock.

"Let me help," I begged. "We'll be fast. I promise."

He came just close enough to drop a kiss on my forehead and then he straightened his jacket so that it hid the worst of it. "I must go, buttercup. I'll see you in an hour or two."

And then he swept his hat off the floor and left the room.

CHAPTER 4

SILAS

I'd lied to Molly.

The moment I closed the door of the rented room, I was searching out another space, one private enough where I could rectify the embarrassing physical situation I found myself in. And the whole time, my mind was screaming *why did you leave her, go back go back go back*, but I knew I couldn't. For one thing, we'd violated the contract. Well, *I* had violated it, despite all of her careful and creative planning last night to find a way for us to share intimacy without breaching the damned thing, and then I'd blown all that work to hell when I'd shoved my fingers inside of her.

While a sick part of me could justify the breach by saying that my actions had only been to take care of her after her confession, no part of me could justify further violating the agreement simply for my own pleasure.

And for another thing, there was her confession itself, and all of the rage and concern and tenderness and frustration it inspired within me. I'd wanted to show her that I was there to support her, there to love her, but I also wanted to respect the solemnity of the moment. The seriousness of it.

Serious and solemn moments, moments filled with tragedy and pain, should only rarely evolve into sticky cum-covered moments.

I wouldn't say never. But *rarely*.

And the very next door I tried opened to my efforts. It was empty, and with a silent prayer, I locked the door and hoped no one would try to return to the room in the next... well, honestly, it wouldn't take very long.

I freed myself as quickly as I could, letting out a long breath when I finally circled my hand around my dick and started pumping. I didn't bother to pull my pants down any farther or even unbutton my jacket; I widened my stance and worked my cock fast and hard, imagining it was Molly's hand wrapped around me, that it was her breathing I heard instead of my own.

I looked down to see the dusky-dark crown pushing through my fingers and then pulling back, disappearing and reappearing, and I thought about how it would look thrusting up between her breasts or between the cheeks of her ass. I tightened my fist, thinking about that ass, about the way she'd gasped and panted when I'd fucked her there for the first time. I'd been gentle and easy since Molly had never allowed a lover to take her that way. Only me. I'd been the first to fuck that hot, tight place. I'd been the first to mark her there.

And then my mind disappeared into a filthy haze of images—some remembered, some imagined—depraved things that I would never admit to thinking in polite company...or even in not-so-polite company. The feeling of Molly's delicate throat under the crush of my fingers, the image of my hand holding her down as I pumped into her.

The tableau of her and me and Viola and—yes, even Castor—all together in that bedroom, slick cunts and warm mouths and hunger. Me straddling Molly and jetting cum onto her lovely freckled face.

I erupted all over my hand, long spurts of white heat, groaning and fucking my fist even faster to spur the pleasure on longer, pretending for those last few thrusts that it really was Molly's cunt I was fucking and not my own hand. Until finally, I stilled, breathing hard. My lust was temporarily slaked, but I didn't feel any better. Instead, I tried to push down the yawning emptiness that wanted to creep up in its place.

I didn't want to do this alone.

I wanted to be with her.

And on top of that, what kind of man needed a woman that way after she'd told him the terrible stories of how someone had abused her?

A *bad* man, that's the kind of man.

I felt a little guilty for using the nearby ewer and towel to clean myself, since this wasn't my room, but it needed to be done. A few minutes (and some vigorous scrubbing) later, I was clean and decent enough to be seen in public. I pressed the emptiness down, along with the anger over what Molly had endured at the hands of that monster, plastered a grin on my face and made my way to the club's dining room.

Generally only members were allowed to dine at the club, but members could invite guests, and since Castor was a member, we were more than welcome. When I reached the table, Julian, Castor and Martjin van der Sant were deeply engaged in a conversation about shifting trade alliances around the Empire. I made my apologies for my lateness, was introduced and sat, staying quiet for most of the meal. Not necessarily because business didn't interest me, but because I wanted to study van der Sant, this man I'd rashly plunged into business with for Molly's sake.

Van der Sant seemed to be the kind of person who inspired respect, not affection. Though short in stature, his rigid posture and imposing demeanor gave the impression of a much larger man, and his conversation was clipped and direct. Completely humorless.

However, when Julian happened to mention his child, van der Sant's face softened. "I always wanted a son," the Dutch man said. "But I am more than pleased with my Birgit."

He turned his attention to the waiter, to signal for more water, while the three of us exchanged uncomfortable glances. Castor and Molly had arranged tonight so that Birgit's innocence would be unequivocal. But we hadn't once given a thought to the emotional toll this would take on van der Sant, witnessing the attempted seduction of his daughter. Would he be furious? Devastated?

How would I feel if this happened to one of my nieces? Or my own daughter? There was no way to endure that kind of test politely or stoically—every protective instinct roared at the thought. In fact, I wanted to go upstairs now and strangle Cunningham before he could even lay eyes on Birgit again.

But of course, reality was slightly more complicated. The illegality of murder aside, there was the issue of preserving the relationship between father and daughter along with Birgit's virtue. I'd not been consulted—perhaps if I had, I would have advised against all this subterfuge and opted for something more direct—but I knew enough about Molly to know that she believed in almost nothing more than the sanctity and warmth of a healthy love between a father and his daughter. I knew enough about Molly to know that she saw Birgit as a younger version of herself, and that her efforts to help Birgit were penances paid to the ghost of the girl Molly used to be.

Lost in thought, I didn't notice how the conversation had shifted until the mention of Molly's name pulled me out of my haze. My head snapped up to see van der Sant gesturing delicately with his fork.

"...Currently investigating a shipping company here in London that we'd like to work with. However, there have been rumors of certain *behaviors*," he said distastefully. "My manager tells me that there are a few people who assert that Miss O'Flaherty has been sighted acting immorally."

Immorally. The word carried judgment and self-righteousness and the strident fervor of someone who associated any and all irregularity in public behavior as a moral failing.

Irritation flared, irritation and the very real urge to drive my fist into van der Sant's face. But that was unthinkable— however harshly he criticized Molly, he was still a potential business partner, and I couldn't jeopardize that with my selfish need to defend her. The company was more important to her than what some priggish stranger thought of her. Aside from that, Molly's relationship with the three of us was still unknown to van der Sant, and it was prudent to keep it that way until it was absolutely unavoidable. It would be wise to keep up the illusion that we were merely investors interested in sealing our exchange with a friendly meal.

He may decide not to do business with Molly at all after tonight, I thought. But that was out of my control. My reaction to van der Sant's statement, however, was in my control. With great effort, I kept my face relaxed and open, my lips tilted up in an interested smile.

But next to me, Castor and Julian had both stiffened, Castor's powerful frame no longer merely athletic but threatening. Silent anger spilled out from Julian, spilling like paraffin oil across the table, a dangerous thing waiting to be kindled into explosive flames.

I glanced over to Castor, whose scowling visage indicated he was ready to fling lightning bolts down upon his enemies, like a muscled, clean-shaven Zeus, and then over to Julian, who flexed and fisted a hand under the table, unconsciously rehearsing for a duel of honor, and then to van der Sant, who seemed baffled by the sudden and stony silence that had fallen over the table. It appeared that it was going to have to be me who kept this dinner afloat, along with Molly's prospective partnership with van der Sant's company.

"Rumors are just that, Mr. van der Sant," I said easily, using the smile that had gotten me dances in the ballroom and reprieves from my childhood nursemaid. "Just words. Did you happen to find anything substantially immoral in the company itself while you were investigating?"

Van der Sant shook his head and wiped his mouth. "That's just it, Mr. Cecil-Coke. The company has been sedulously guided through the years. The books are scrupulously kept, the managers are all honest, and there's been nothing irregular whatsoever in the financial machinery of her business."

"Surely that is a better testament to Miss O'Flaherty's character than mere hearsay?" I asked, lifting an eyebrow.

"I'm forced to concede you are correct," van der Sant admitted. "And while I find it improper for a woman to be involved in a man's enterprise to begin with, I cannot ignore that she's done a marvelous job. Her company still presents an excellent opportunity for us, and though it may trouble my conscience, I believe I will put aside those rumors permanently. Ultimately, what matters is that her company is ethically run, and in that respect, it is spotless."

Good, you asshole, was what I wanted to say. But I

refrained, instead only making a small noise of approval in my throat and then asking if he'd like more wine.

Next to me, Castor and Julian slowly let go of their anger, and by the time we were finished with the meal, a semblance of civility had covered over the earlier tension. Still, Julian's voice was brusque when he stood and said, "Would you like to retire with us upstairs for some brandy? Silas and I would like to talk over our new investment."

Van der Sant nodded. "Of course."

The room wasn't empty when we opened the door. Of course, that was the plan, but I still felt a clench of anxiety when Molly stood and swept toward Birgit's father with a serious look creasing her face. I wanted to protect her from this—all of it. From van der Sant's disapproval, from the memories of Cunningham's touch, from the chaos that could ensue after Cunningham's perversion was exposed.

But Molly didn't need protecting. With her shoulders back and her eyes slightly narrowed in determination and her dress gleaming green in the light of the small chandelier and its matching wall sconces, she looked like a solemn figure from some sort of Gaelic myth.

"I'm so glad you're here," she said quietly to Martjin van der Sant. "I have something important to discuss with you."

The Dutch man looked from me to Castor to Julian—and then back to Molly—confused and clearly a little annoyed. "Miss O'Flaherty, this is highly unusual. And improper."

"It's about Birgit," she interrupted, politely but firmly. "It's about your daughter."

This was enough to halt whatever he'd been prepared to say next. Concern flashed in his eyes. "Please explain."

Only I saw the way Molly's chest rose, as if she was taking in a breath for courage but also trying to hide it. I thought of her earlier today, her hand trembling in mine, her eyes glittering with unshed tears. *It's too late for me.*

I'd tried to prove to her that it wasn't; that nothing changed the way I felt about her. If anything, I loved her even more, not because her story inspired me to protect her and heal her, but because it had allowed me a glimpse of the incalculable strength of her mind, the diamond-hard quintessence of her soul. It allowed me to see a Molly that I saw rarely—a woman both fragile and fierce, brilliant and yet so impossibly ignorant about herself.

I love you, I thought fervently, trying to send that thought to her, to strengthen her.

And maybe it worked. She let go of the breath she'd held and answered in that same calm but firm voice. "When I first met Birgit, I asked her to consider me a friend. After all, we are both very similar—we were both raised by fathers after our mothers had died. Our fathers were both prosperous businessman. And both of us were deeply loved by these fathers."

Molly had said the right thing. Van der Sant's irritation melted somewhat, and he nodded.

She went on. "In addition, I wanted to extend my protection to her. Birgit is very beautiful and very young and very...untouched. I'm sad to say that I know from personal experience that a man within my own company is drawn to such girls. I worried that Birgit would capture his eye, and I wanted to make sure that he couldn't bring any harm to her, as he has to me and others. Unfortunately, she came to me this morning to tell me that he has threatened her with the most appalling of arrangements. That she must surrender herself to him or he will publicly slander her reputation. He has told her that if she doesn't comply with his wishes then he'll convince you that she's been dishonest and unchaste."

"That's a very concerning allegation," van der Sant said after a pause.

"I know it is," she agreed. "And it probably seems unlikely. Outlandish even. Which is why I am not asking you to believe me without proof." She indicated the corner of the room, where a narrow door was set into the wall, a remnant from a century ago, when this building had been a family house. There was a heavy table placed against it to discourage use, and indeed, it looked like no one had touched it in decades, but a door it remained, and it allowed eavesdropping, provided you pressed your ear to the seam and listened closely.

Van der Sant seemed to grasp Molly's meaning right away. Color rose up his neck, anger and horror and disbelief. "Are you—is my daughter behind that door?"

His anger didn't faze Molly. "She will be shortly. The room adjoining us belongs to Frederick Cunningham."

"Mr. Cunningham," he said. "He's the man you were referring to?"

"Yes."

Van der Sant's mouth opened and closed at this new piece of information. Molly forged on. "I can understand why you are angry. Why this situation infuriates you. But before you vent your rage on me and before you storm into the next room, I want you to know that Birgit sincerely believes that you would not put faith in her if she came to you. Your own daughter, who adores you and has never given you any reason to doubt her, still thinks that you do not love and trust her enough to believe her story."

Van der Sant's neck grew redder, as did his cheeks and ears. "That's preposterous," he said, his voice growing louder.

"My daughter knows she has my full trust. She should have come to me and not a…strange woman!"

"Think," Molly ordered. "Would you really? If your daughter came to you and claimed something so heinous about a man you had chosen to do business with? What would you really think?"

Van der Sant seemed ready to yell again, but he didn't. He met Molly's eyes instead, his gaze blazing full of indignation, his jaw working as if he were picking precisely the right words to say. But Molly didn't blink or look away.

"There's nothing to be gained from lying to yourself," she said, a bit sternly. "You're a hard man, Mr. van der Sant. A good man, maybe, but a hard one. Even to your daughter."

He stared at Molly for another minute, the red slowly receding from his cheeks. He finally dropped his eyes to the floor. "That's possibly not untrue." The concession cost him visible effort.

Encouraged, Molly stepped even closer. "Will you please allow us to prove Birgit's innocence? So we can extract her from this terrible situation?"

Van der Sant was clearly torn. The plan seemed so reckless and terrible at first—even I had felt that way—but under the surface, Castor and Molly had planned for every eventuality. I listened as she explained to him that Castor's men were shadowing Cunningham until he came to his room, that Castor's most trusted servant was escorting Birgit here to ensure that she remained safe until she reached her destination. And once both Cunningham and Birgit entered, we would be able to hear through the door if Birgit cried for help, in which circumstance, Castor's men would break into the room and rescue her.

After the explanations were complete, van der Sant found a chair and sat down, rubbing at his forehead. It was the only fissure in his perfect self-control that I could see, but I suspected that with a man like him, the smallest ripple in his disciplined mien signaled tremendous turbulence underneath.

"I am still troubled that my daughter did not come to me first," he said, but there was less recrimination in his voice now, less superiority. "But I suppose I understand why she felt she could not."

Three light knocks on the door. The signal that Cunningham was inside his room. By some unspoken cue, we all quieted, even van der Sant, who seemed as if he still had more he wanted to say.

Not five minutes later, there were four knocks at the door. Birgit was now in the lion's den.

CHAPTER 5

MOLLY

*I*t made me sick.

Even though Castor and I had been so careful, even though every angle had been thought through to achieve both our goals—keeping Birgit safe *and* extricating her from Cunningham's trap without endangering her relationship with her father—it still felt wrong. Wrong and despicable, to let her alone in a room with a man like him.

Van der Sant was standing with his ear pressed against the seam, as were Castor and Julian, but Silas had found his way to me in the middle of the room, where I stood wondering if I should go over there. Silas's hand slipped in mine, something van der Sant would probably find deeply inappropriate if he were watching, which he wasn't.

Silas squeezed my fingers. "Do you want to go over there?"

I nodded, but I still couldn't move. It was only when I heard a low growl of anger from Castor that I knew I needed to hear what he was hearing. I was, for all intents and purposes, the author of this situation and I needed to see it through to the end. No matter how many painful and shameful memories were dredged up in the process.

The men rearranged themselves slightly, and I found a place to listen. There was silence at first, and for a moment, I panicked that perhaps he was forcing her right this minute and she hadn't managed to give any sort of signal, but then there was the clinking of glass against glass and deliberate footsteps.

"I don't drink," came Birgit's muffled voice.

"It will help you relax," Cunningham urged. I hated that voice, that voice that pretended he was being kind and attentive even as he forced you against your will. Like everything he did—even the defilement—was for your best interest and any protest on your part came from ignorance or petulance. Like you were just a selfish child and he was the patient adult trying to coax you into doing what you were supposed to do.

"I'd really rather not," she insisted. "My father doesn't approve of women drinking."

"Your father isn't here, is he?"

Van der Sant didn't react, at least on the surface. There was a slight twitch to one eye, a careful rhythm to his breathing that told me he was trying to maintain complete control and that it was costing him significant effort.

"No," Birgit said, and even through the door, I could hear the trembling in her voice. The fear. I swallowed, trying to stop the ball tightening in my throat as I felt my own fear again, my own remembered panic on the day Cunningham took my body and a piece of my soul.

You are not that girl anymore.

It was true. I'd worked so hard to make sure that my body was my own, that my sex was my own. That Molly only belonged to herself and not to the ghosts of the past. But that girl would always be there, somewhere, hiding inside of me. Waiting for the right events to bring her shivering and crying to the fore.

Cunningham murmured something, and Birgit cleared her throat loudly, launching into the script we'd rehearsed.

"Please, Mr. Cunningham, I don't want to do this."

"What you want doesn't matter, Miss van der Sant. I think you know that already."

"I don't want to—" her voice broke off, thick with tears, and my own tears were coming now, welling up and clinging to my eyelashes.

"If you don't give me what I want, I will ruin you. You understand that, right? I can ruin you. And now that you're here—well, I'm afraid you don't have much of a choice. You *will* do what I want, and no one will believe you if you try to tell them."

No one will believe you. Wasn't that what I had told myself all these years? Why I'd kept his crimes a secret? Because who would believe the word of a woman over the word of a gentleman like him?

Except I could see how imprisoning that belief had been; maybe not everybody would have believed me, maybe not the public at large, but here were my three closest friends and all of them had plunged themselves into this situation to help as soon as they learned about it. They'd all believed me about Birgit. And they would have believed me about my own story. Warmth seeped in through the shame, not erasing it necessarily, but making it lighter, smaller. As if knowing what I felt, Silas wrapped an arm around my waist, and both Julian and Castor looked up at me with such expressions of friendship and trust that my tears did truly spill over. Julian frowned—he still didn't know about Cunningham—only Silas knew how personally this affected me, how difficult it was for me to stand here and not relive every awful moment of my own torture. But I knew that if I told him, he would be exactly what I needed. Kind but not overbearing. Concerned but not pitying.

While I pondered this, the conversation had continued on the other side of the door. More of Cunningham's evil words and more of Birgit's tears, until finally van der Sant straightened abruptly. "I've heard enough," he said tightly, and Castor was at the door in an instant to summon his men.

And then there were shouts, tables and chairs knocking over in a scuffle; and then Birgit was in her father's arms, and the stoic Martjin van der Sant finally succumbed to the anger and pain he'd repressed all evening, sobbing into his daughter's neck and apologizing profusely for whatever he'd done to make her doubt his love under any circumstance; and then the constables were called, and then there was Castor giving testimony along with van der Sant and Birgit herself, and Cunningham was brought away and I stood in the hallway as he passed.

"*You*," he hissed as they dragged him away.

"Me," I said. And the look he shot me was venomous enough to kill, but he couldn't kill me in any sense any longer. He was finally exposed. He would be punished. And the part of me that was still sixteen, still a terrified girl pretending to be brave, breathed a sigh of relief and closed her eyes at last.

"YOU'RE SHIVERING," Silas said.

I was. In fact, I wasn't even sure how we'd ended up in this carriage that was currently rattling me back to my house. Silas must have called for it…what had happened to the others? I vaguely remembered van der Sant wanting a physician to tend to Birgit's nerves, Castor thundering words to the constables, who scrambled to obey the aristocrat, Julian clutching one of my arms while Silas clutched the other, and him murmuring to Silas, and Silas murmuring back over my head.

"I don't know what's wrong with me," I said, my teeth chattering. My hands shook so hard that I couldn't even try to untie the bonnet I'd put on at some point.

"Catharsis," Silas said in a gentle voice. "You're purging something you've carried for a long time. You had to feel it all again, confront it all again, and now you're able to let go of it."

My shivering was so violent that I couldn't even respond, and the tears came again. Silas moved over to my seat and crushed me against his chest.

And then we were home, and then he was carrying me, and then we were in my bed, fully clothed, his body curled protectively around mine, and I felt only a weary sort of peace as I slipped into a dreamless sleep.

When I woke, I woke up alone. I knew why Silas had felt so betrayed when I'd left him the other day; falling asleep in his arms had felt so deeply right that waking up and finding nothing next to me felt deeply wrong.

I sat up, aching and stiff from having slept in my clothes, and found a note on the side table.

I've stepped out to check on a few business matters. I'll call on you later today.

I set the note aside, feeling a grim sort of reality settle in. Would it really be wise to have Silas call on me? We'd spent so much of the last day together, it was impossible that Hugh wouldn't hear about it. And while Cunningham was now out of the picture, I had no guarantee that the rest of the board wouldn't still insist upon my marriage to Hugh. And I was certain that my successful rescue of Birgit had also cost my company the partnership with van der Sant's. There was no way he would want to continue working with us. So I'd done nothing to help myself and possibly even hurt my company with my actions yesterday.

But I couldn't regret them. In fact, despite my pragmatic view of the current situation, I still felt a sense of victory. A sense of completion. I'd done the right thing. I'd protected Birgit and I'd seen justice done to Cunningham. And maybe that was worth my bleak future.

Treasures in heaven... That's what the priest in Ennis used to preach about when I was a girl. So I wouldn't have treasures on earth. At least I'd done moral good in the world... maybe God would look at that and not at my hedonistic past when I died.

A knock sounded at the door. My lady's maid came in, carrying a freshly pressed dress. "It's time to dress, miss. And don't forget that the dressmaker will be calling later today for your final fitting."

The dressmaker. For the engagement ball. Which was —*fuck*—tomorrow night.

"Of course," I said calmly, although inside I was twisting with unhappiness. "I wouldn't miss it for the world."

SILAS

Molly was out when I came to her house. She'd gone to visit Birgit van der Sant, her butler intoned sternly, and he didn't know when she'd be back. He also made a point to tell me that Hugh was expected for dinner.

I sometimes got the feeling her butler didn't like me very much.

I went back to my townhouse and paced my parlor floor for several long hours, until I finally gave up and went to

Castor's, where I held Julian's baby until I felt better, missing my nieces and nephews. Missing my family. Missing Molly.

Only I could manage to feel lonely in the busiest, most important city in the world.

The next day dawned foggy and gray, mist clinging to trees just this side of turning colors, and the first thing I did after waking was seek out my solicitor. I knew it was early to expect confirmation for our shares, but I also wanted to know what was going on with Molly's board. Were they still determined to see her married? Were they shaken up by Cunningham's arrest? Had everything changed for the better?

Or the worse?

The Cecil-Coke solicitor was named Kestwick, an imposing man of equally imposing age, white hair and wrinkles upon wrinkles, with a posture and strength that belied his years. He rose to shake my hand when I entered his office, and then we both sat.

"Have we had confirmation yet?" I asked without preamble.

"I expect it any hour. I'll send word as soon as I hear," he promised.

I frowned. I wanted that confirmation before Molly's engagement ball tonight. I wanted her all to myself, I didn't want her dancing with Hugh tonight, standing with him, pretending to be happy with him. The thought infuriated me.

I changed the subject, trying to step away from my anger, which wasn't really directed at anybody but Hugh. "Any word about Cunningham's arrest?"

Kestwick raised his eyebrows. "You must be joking."

My frown deepened. "I'm not really in a joking mood," I said.

"It's all anybody is talking about. So far, it looks as if the charges are serious enough that he will be imprisoned for quite a long time. Martjin van der Sant is bringing every ounce of influence and money he has against Cunningham, and the rumor is that the court is disposed to side entirely with the van der Sants."

I nodded. "Good." It was still difficult to understand why Cunningham had been so foolish, so caught up in his perversion that he sought out a girl so powerfully connected, but I supposed it was a mixture of overconfidence and lust.

And if I had my way, the man would be murdered in jail for what he had done to Molly, but I wouldn't worry about that right now. Right now, I could only think about preventing this terrible marriage from moving forward.

"Unfortunately, the board of O'Flaherty Shipping has not changed its position on Miss O'Flaherty's marriage. However," he said, leaning forward, "as this matter with their leader grows inevitably more sordid, I believe that several of the members will be more interested in selling their shares."

"To distance themselves from the scandal," I said. "Let's hope that happens, and if it does, I want to be there to buy them immediately."

Kestwick nodded. "It will be so."

"Good." I got out of the chair and we shook hands once again. "Don't forget—the minute you hear the confirmation."

"Yes. You'll be notified as quickly as humanly possible."

And with that paltry assurance, I left and went to pick out a suit to wear to the ball celebrating the engagement of the woman I loved to another man.

CHAPTER 6

MOLLY

*D*resses get their magic from different places. Some dresses are magic because of where they are worn, a place that holds romance and potential and happiness. Some dresses are magic because of the people they affect—a bridal gown that brings a bridegroom to tears, for example.

And some dresses are magic simply because of the dress they are. The magic is in the fabric and the pleats themselves, the tiny stitches and even seams.

Tonight my dress was magic, even though I felt like I was wearing it to my doom. It was a bold choice for a soon-to-be bride, but I didn't care. I wanted bold, I wanted it to scream *Molly O'Flaherty*. I wanted the eyes of the ballroom on me one last time before I tumbled headlong into this terrible marriage.

It was red, the kind of red that poets write about, a red that was bright and vivid and deep all at once, a red that brought to mind blood and roses and cherries hanging ripe on a tree. The silk glistened like scarlet water in the light, clinging to my curves and spilling out behind me in a glorious bustle with a small train. Coupled with my hair piled high with curls gracefully draped over one shoulder and a sheer red shawl hanging from my arms, there would be no mistaking me. No opportunity to paint me as some meek blushing bride. My last act of defiance to Hugh and my last chance to feel beautiful on my own terms.

I went to find a necklace to pair with it, settling on a small gold chain with a ruby cross. Though I'd purchased it in Rome with my own money, something about it always reminded me of my aunt back in Ennis. Maybe it was the cross—despite her aberrant views on pregnancy and fertility, she'd been quite religious. Or maybe it was the rubies, which reminded me of the dark red helleborine flowers that grew around her house. Either way, I pressed my hand against the cross, missing her cottage, missing *her*, the woman who was so like her sister, my mother.

And then, *shit*, the realization that I hadn't drank my tea today, the tea that my aunt had taught me how to prepare in order to avoid pregnancy. I drank it every morning, and had since I was a girl, but I'd been so exhausted from the week's events that I'd slept clean through breakfast, and pushed away lunch when it was brought to me.

It's fine. You weren't planning on sleeping with Hugh tonight anyway. He'd have to wait until we were actually married for that, and when that happened, I'd make sure to drink the tea every day. Twice a day, maybe.

It would be fine.

With a final glance at the mirror, I went downstairs to meet my fiancé.

❧

THE BALL WAS ABSOLUTELY the largest party I'd ever been to, including the one hosted by the Prince of Orange that Julian and I had attended in Amsterdam one year. Tonight, hundreds of people danced, drank, and flirted, all of them coming to the front to greet Hugh and me.

I have so many friends, I realized with a sense of sadness. For so long, I'd kept myself apart—burdened by my secrets, consumed by my business. Coming out to play whenever I needed a distraction. And all along, these people had grown attached to me, fond of me, even though I'd been distant and frequently dismissive. Possibly even cruel.

All of these friends, all of this carefree joy and light-hearted laughter as they drank and ate (at my expense, but that was easily forgiven)—would it all vanish once I was legally under Hugh's thumb?

Unlike me, my future husband was untroubled by any sort of introspection or epiphany. He laughed along with the guests, handsome, ruddy, and blond, a picture of Saxon health and vitality. He shook hands and he kissed hands. He bowed to women and he embraced men.

Unlike me, he had nothing but a happy future ahead. A rich wife, an infusion of money, and nothing else about his life would have to change.

It took everything I had not to push him away whenever he drew me close. Especially when *that woman* Mercy Atworth sashayed up to us, her dark hair glistening and her neckline low. Mercy had driven Silas and me apart last year —and almost again last month—and while I tried to remember that it wasn't necessarily any fault of her own, since I had never laid public stake to Silas and Silas was by far the guiltier party when it came to both of those incidents, it was hard not to hate her. Her and her easy beauty and her lush sexuality.

We'd been friends once. More than friends; I knew what

her nipples felt like hardening against my tongue. I knew what sounds she made when she came around my fingers. But that was a lifetime ago, in another world, with another Molly. Now I kept my posture stiff and restrained as she curtsied to us both. And then Hugh pulled her in to kiss her cheeks, both kisses landing at the edge of her curved, full mouth.

There was something about their familiarity that scratched at me—it wasn't jealousy, not at all, although if Silas had touched her that way, I would have dug my fingers into her eyes until I touched her brain.

No, it was more like the realization that the two of them were closer than I'd really understood. Close like the closest friends, sensual like the most passionate lovers.

It struck me that the way they stood right now, hands clasped, bodies tilted toward one another's like twin plants arcing toward the same sunbeam, was a lot like how Silas and I were around one another.

Were Hugh and Mercy…*in love?*

This didn't upset me. This didn't even change my perception that Hugh was genuinely fond of me, in a romantic way. I knew better than most people that you could believe yourself in love with one person while you were actually deeply and subconsciously in love with another.

I turned this new angle on their friendship over in my mind as she chattered with Hugh. I thought of how close they were, how frequently they spent time with one another. I thought of something else too. I thought of Hugh's anxious displeasure when Silas came to town. Of the day we'd caught Silas with his cock inside Mercy's mouth. I'd been with Hugh, lunching together in his townhouse, when he'd received a brief letter from Mercy. "She needs us to stop by," he'd said, folding the letter and tucking it into his jacket. And I'd agreed to go, not needing to be anywhere else.

So it had been no coincidence that we'd walked in to find that scene. Which made me feel marginally better about Silas's role in that, but quite depressed about my own intelligence. How had I not seen the trap? How had I not seen how I'd been guided and manipulated—not just by Hugh and Mercy, but by Cunningham and the board? For all these months...all these years?

I snagged a glass off of a tray traveling nearby, draining the champagne in two easy swallows. I scanned the room for Silas—something I'd been doing approximately every three or four minutes since the ball started. Castor was here, as were Julian and Ivy, and everyone else we knew.

But not Silas.

Not that I could blame him. If he were throwing himself a massive ball to celebrate his engagement to someone else, I wouldn't be able to go either. But it still stung, because I missed him. I craved him. Especially after what I'd shared with him; he was one of the few people in the world who knew all of me, and the only one who loved me the way I needed to be loved. I knew this had to be unbearable for him, but what about me?

Doesn't anyone care that it's unbearable for me?

The time came for a toast, led by Gideon, Hugh's closest friend. I allowed my thoughts to wander during his speech, pretending to laugh and smile at all the right jokes, and then it was time for Hugh and me to dance. The band struck up a tune, Hugh found my hand and my waist, and then we were spinning around the dance floor, our partygoers forming a circle around us.

Hugh smiled down at me, and I once again appreciated how completely oblivious he was to everything—my feelings, my needs, the unique monstrosity of the situation. And I couldn't stand it anymore. That smug happiness needed to end, and given that this was the first time we'd had anything remotely approximating a private conversation since the other morning, it was going to end now.

Why not start off this miserable union from a place of total honesty?

As we moved toward the center of the room, well out of earshot of our guests, I looked up at Hugh. "I know that Cunningham is your cousin," I informed him.

It took a moment for Hugh to process this, his smile slowly fading and his shoulder growing tense under my hand. "You know?"

I sensed that he was searching for a defense, a justification, for keeping something like this from me, which of course there was no acceptable justification. "I know that you have no money. I know that Cunningham has been lending you enough to keep you living at a certain standard. And I know that you deliberately kept this fact from me."

Hugh chewed on the inside of his mouth for a moment before slipping back into his easy smile. "Molly, you must understand. Frederick and I knew it would complicate something that was so simple—and complicate it unnecessarily. We were—*are*—such a good match, and we didn't want you to be distracted by that one small facet of our connection."

I gave him a smile back, but I knew it was in no way easy, that it was a hard, sharp smile. "There is no *we*, when it comes to you and Cunningham anymore, I'm afraid."

Hugh tensed again. "I'm aware," he said tightly. He could hardly not be—his cousin's arrest was prime gossip in every fashionable club and ballroom in London, along with rumors of all his perversions.

"I did it," I told him, still wearing my sharp smile. "I didn't know if you knew that. I made sure your cousin was caught and arrested before he could hurt another girl."

Hugh's hand tightened around mine, painfully so, but I didn't lose the smile. Fury pooled in his rich brown eyes. And perhaps I was digging my own grave, perhaps I was making things worse for myself after our wedding, but I *didn't care*. Somewhere in the last two days, I'd been freed from caring. All that mattered was Hugh knowing that I *knew*. That out of everything, he couldn't claim that victory.

"And you and Mercy? I know that you arranged that scenario with Silas."

"He was a willing participant within that scenario," Hugh hissed. We were whirling back by the guests again, and he struggled to keep his voice low. "He wasn't doing anything he didn't want to do."

"I agree. But I also think it was truly wretched of you to make me witness it."

"Perhaps not any more wretched than you seeing my cousin thrown in jail on such ridiculous charges." This brown eyes were practically embers now; I could feel their scalding heat.

I ignored it. "That you think Cunningham's behavior doesn't merit punishment is one of the worst things about you."

Hugh yanked me closer to him, forcing me to stumble in my steps and balance against his chest. "I hope you've enjoyed your little outburst, Molly. Because, believe me, after we are married, I won't allow it to happen again."

And then the music ended, Hugh's ominous words hanging in the air as we separated. But I didn't mind. I'd reached a place of utter numbness, of not caring, because what consequences could be worse than anything else I'd already endured? I floated away from Hugh and the dance floor, disappearing into the crowd as they swarmed back in pairs to dance and drink and twirl under the chandeliers as if they didn't have a care in the world.

I slipped through them all, feeling drunk on my numbness, feeling—in a sick way—proud of my stoic forbearance and practicality in the face of my new life. And now I would go find some gin and become actually drunk, and maybe I would fall asleep before I had to endure any more of this terrible party. When I glanced over one shoulder, I saw Hugh and Mercy dancing together, Mercy looking characteristically congenial in her sultry way, Hugh whispering furiously to her...no doubt relating all of the things I'd just told him.

I was insensate to it all. In fact, I was grateful for their camaraderie. Maybe they'd fuck each other and I'd avoid Hugh's inevitable advances, which tonight would no doubt be laced with menace. I turned back to my path, searching for gin the way that a falcon searches for a mouse in the field.

I narrowed in on a waiter in the corner of the room, who was carefully pouring drinks. As he hoisted his tray into the air and moved into the fray and bustle of the crowd, I brushed past his station, swiping the decanter of gin. Then I ducked between two thick curtains by a window nearby, relishing the cool air seeping through the glass. The window was deeply inset into the wall, enough that I could step easily behind the curtains without feeling too claustrophobic. I wasn't completely hidden, but I was mostly obscured from view and I had gin, so that was good enough for now.

I took a swig straight from the decanter, savoring the botanical burn as it traveled down my throat, and then the decanter was lifted from my fingers.

"I've found the blushing bride, I see," Silas said.

I turned. "You're here," I whispered, joy clawing up my chest like pain. "You came."

He took his own drink from the decanter and then set it gently on the waist-high windowsill. "Yes. I came."

I licked my lips—an unconscious response to his nearness, his maleness, as he took a step closer to me. His clean Silas smell came over me, soap and citrus and gin, and his eyes dropped down to my mouth as I bit my lower lip.

"Where's Hugh?" Silas asked.

"He's off dancing. With—" I waved a hand, the gin suddenly making the world brighter and fuzzier. "—With Mercy."

Silas blanched a little at Mercy's name, a blanch of guilt and regret, but he quickly recovered. "Good. I want you to myself right now."

I glanced around. "I don't know if that's a good idea. Somebody might see."

"Mary Margaret, I would love it if someone saw." Something in his tone made me look back to him as heat flooded between my legs. His voice was a low growl when he said, "I want them to see me take what's mine."

Oh, God. It was *this* Silas, and I was helpless against this Silas, numb or not numb. My newfound pseudo-peace as an automaton resigned to her fate slowly filtered away, replaced by a liquid warmth pouring into my core.

"But Hugh," I protested weakly as Silas walked behind me, wrapped an arm around my waist, and tugged me deeper into the recess formed by the heavy, pleated curtains. "The contract."

"They don't matter anymore," he said sternly. "What matters is you giving me what I want." One arm wrapped around my waist as his long fingers wound in my hair and yanked my head back. "What's your safe word?"

I took a deep breath, almost unable to cope with the feeling of his body behind me, crushing up against my dress. Of his hands in my hair. Of his words at my ear.

If you acknowledge this, if you whisper your safe word, then you're agreeing to submit to him...you're agreeing to this.

I knew that if I kept up my protests, however weak they may be, that Silas wouldn't cross the line. What happened in The Hedgehog that night had been inspired by my confession, by my pain, and I knew he wouldn't abet me in breaching my contract again.

But.

If I acknowledged my safe word, it was a very clear signal that I was willing to let him take me. It was also a concession that all the power rested with me. I alone would be responsible for stopping us before things went too far; it would be me who had to decide when to stop, not Silas's sense of gentlemanly conduct.

I shouldn't say anything. I should walk away. As tipsy as I was, as weary and tired as I was, I still knew the consequences of breaching my contract would be too disastrous to endure. If Hugh caught me—not an unlikely scenario, given that Silas and I were barely hidden in this obscenely crowded ballroom —then I could lose all rights to my company. And I couldn't bear that. Not after I'd fought so hard and sacrificed so much.

But then Silas pressed me closer, his fingers moving from my hair to my neck, and I shivered, thrills skating across my skin. There was something so dangerous and primal about Silas's fascination with my neck, as if he couldn't help but test his strength against me, as if the feeling of my pulse beneath his fingers was the most potent aphrodisiac in the world.

"I asked you a question," he growled in my ear.

I had to make a choice. Did I trust Silas? Did I want him? Did I love him enough to give him myself right now, so publicly, so dangerously? Or did I do what I'd done for the last year, and put the company first?

Always the company.

Fuck the company.

The thought came from nowhere, but it came as clear as a church bell through the cool morning air.

Fuck the company.

Hadn't it taken enough? Hadn't I given it everything—my time, my happiness, my future—and even still, it wasn't secure? I would marry Hugh, but I only had a tentative verbal agreement that I would get to remain in charge of the company; if Hugh wanted, he could dismantle the company at a moment's notice. Legally, as his wife, my life's work would belong to him and I would have no recourse. Was that what Aiden O'Flaherty really would have wanted for his daughter?

No.

I chose Silas. I chose my future. Perhaps it was the gin or the warm press of his body or the feeling of his fingers just barely denting the skin of my throat, but everything in me rebelled against the bleak future I'd built for myself and clamored for something different. For the man I loved.

"Clare," I said finally.

CHAPTER 7

SILAS

*C*lare.

So many meanings for such a small word. For her, it meant home and her mother and a future she could only dream of. And for me, it meant *Molly*. It meant her body under mine, my palm stinging against her ass, her blue eyes wide and dark as her body shuddered with a climax that I'd given her.

With my hand cupped around her throat, I *felt* her speak her next words more than I heard them.

"What did you say, Mary Margaret?" I murmured.

"You," she repeated, louder this time. I loosened my grip so that she could turn in my arms and face me. "I choose you."

My pulse sped up and my heart crashed against my ribs. *Be cautious. Be sure.* After what Molly had been through, I had to let her make this decision on her own. I wouldn't push her, although I wanted to. I wanted to guide her, to coax her, to force her to admit that she wanted me and only me and that nothing was worth letting us go.

But I wouldn't. Because I loved her, because I respected her, because I knew why her company was important to her. If she'd been any different, any less driven and fiercely independent, then she wouldn't have been my Molly.

She slid her hands up my stomach, resting them flat on my chest, and I felt her touch reverberate everywhere along my body. "I don't want to marry Hugh," she said. "I don't want to spend another moment apart from you, and maybe it's the gin talking, but damn the consequences. Damn the company. If that's the price I have to pay to be your Molly, then I'll pay it gladly." Her eyes searched mine, sapphire in the low light of the ballroom. "I love you. I think, in a way, I always have. The night we met in Paris, do you remember?"

Julian and I had brought her to our hotel room and fucked her together, him coming in her mouth and me coming inside of her. I *definitely* remembered.

"We fell asleep together," she continued. "You and me, snuggled close while Julian slept on the other side of the bed. It was the first time I'd ever slept with a lover—man or woman. Some part of me must have known, even then, that I was meant to be with you."

My grip on her tightened again, and I leaned in to kiss her. "I love you," I said against her lips. "I love your mind and your cunt and that smile that hardly anyone ever gets to see." She moved her lips to mine, but I pulled back ever so slightly. "I want to hear you say it again. Say that you choose me. Say it."

"I choose you." It was a breath, just whispered syllables against my mouth, but those syllables meant everything. Having this, her choice, her apparent willingness to walk away from everything simply to be with me, wasn't something I expected. And it wasn't something I would have consciously wanted. But now I knew it was something I *needed*, confirmation that her yearning for me was as great as mine was for her.

And the best part was yet to come. I pulled back. "Molly, I need to tell you something. And I know you're going to be furious with me, but I just hope that when I explain why I did it, you'll eventually forgive me."

She tensed in my arms.

"Julian and I didn't just invest in van der Sant's company. We invested in yours too."

"What?"

I kept going, before she could hoist her defenses any higher. "We knew there was a possibility even after you married Hugh that something could go awry with O'Flaherty Shipping, and we didn't want you to be without allies inside the company. Together, Julian and I acquired about twenty percent of the shares."

Still tense and suspicious, I saw her retreat into her mind to run through the calculations. "So between the three of us, we have almost forty percent of the shares," she said slowly. "Still less than half, but not an insignificant number."

I found her face with my hands, forcing her away from her mental ledger and back to me. "It won't be easy if the other shareholders leave, Molly. But you could still salvage the company."

She worried her lip between her teeth. "Maybe. *If* van der Sant still agrees to partner with my company. And that's a big 'if,' given what Cunningham did."

"Or we can sell everything and move to an Irish cottage by the sea. I will do whatever you want, Mary Margaret: if you want to leave and start fresh or stay here and fight. I will be by your side."

Her blue eyes seemed to melt, less sapphires now and more evening sky. "I know you would."

"So you're not angry with me? For trying to 'rescue' you?"

She gave me a rueful smile. "Not this time. But don't make it a habit."

Relief rushed through me. Still holding on to her face, I demanded, "Say it one more time."

"I choose you."

I choose you.

My dick was still half-hard from our gin-flavored kisses, and now it was thickening again. For her. I angled her head to expose her neck, biting hard at the delicate skin there, moving down to her collarbone and shoulder, marking her with my teeth in the same bruising way she'd marked my heart.

"Mine," I half-muttered, half-growled as I bit the tops of her breasts, which were pushed into firm swells by her corset. "Mine."

"Yes," she breathed, her fingers twining in my hair, and with a rumble deep inside my chest, I spun her around so that her back was to the window and I pushed her against it, lifting her onto the deep windowsill.

With no preamble, I started rucking up her skirt, and when I glanced up at her face, her sweet little mouth was parted into an O and her eyes had started to fall shut.

"People might see us," I said, pushing back the layers of silk that separated us.

"I know," she said raggedly, because my hands had just found the soft skin above her stockings.

"I hope they do see us." My voice was vicious and wild. "I hope they see me fucking you. I hope they see as you come from my touch. Because then there can be no mistake. Molly O'Flaherty belongs to *me*. Only me."

She nodded eagerly, a flush creeping up her chest, and I brushed against the wet, hot entrance between her legs. I'd meant what I said: I honestly didn't care that this window was only half hidden. That if a partygoer somehow wandered to this seemingly abandoned corner, they would see the soon-to-be bride getting fucked by someone who wasn't her fiancé. I didn't care that this wasn't the Baron's, that most of these guests were part of London high society and were uninitiated into the libertine life Molly and I had led up until now. I didn't care that they might be shocked. And while I did care about Molly's reputation, I cared more about having her. Claiming her. Sealing our new understanding with a branding, scorching fuck.

"Spread your legs," I ordered. "Spread them wide."

I loved the way she shivered and exhaled when I used that voice, that voice that came so naturally around her. I loved the way she so quickly complied, my fierce fighting Molly, as if there was not a single part of her that could resist obeying me, even though in the other parts of her life, she obeyed no one.

I rubbed myself through my pants as I watched her—her low, silk heels braced against the sill, her white stockings clinging to her delicious legs, ending at the middle of her sweetly freckled thighs. And those perfect thighs opened to that even more perfect cunt, the legs and the cunt both framed by the spill of ruby red silk around her waist.

I squatted for a moment, bringing my face down to the level of her sex, and I leaned in for one taste—just one— licking from the soft place just above her ass all the way up to her clit. And then, unable to resist, I ran the tip of my tongue around the inner folds of her pussy, teasing it in and out of her as she squirmed. I wanted to consume her, drink her and eat her, breathe her and absorb her, and I promised myself soon—*maybe even our wedding night*, this stupidly romantic and hopeful part of me suggested—I would spend hours with my face between her legs doing just that.

"So good," I told her, standing and reaching for the

buttons of my pants. I didn't bother to wipe her taste off my lips—I wanted it there, and I wanted *her* to taste it when I kissed her. I wanted that feeling of her tasting herself as I pushed inside of her, as if I were returning her own pleasure to her, returning her desire back with something added, a circle of completion coupled with something more.

A *spiral*, I realized as my cock fell free from my pants and I leaned in for a kiss. It wasn't a circle at all, because the moment we came back to where we started, I wanted her more. I *loved* her more. And so there wasn't completion, not really, not while we still had breath in our bodies. It was more like we brought each other higher or further, like each fuck and each kiss and each shared look was another twist of the screw that was slowly and painfully and wonderfully affixing our hearts to one another's.

"Silas," she said, her pupils dilated but one eyebrow arching up in impatience. Aroused but scornful: that was pretty much the essence of Molly O'Flaherty. "Please," she added after a minute, although her tone still suggested that she was about to take matters into her own hands (as it were.) "Please fuck me."

Well, what gentleman can say *no* to a lady?

Especially when she asks so politely?

I wrapped my fingers around the base of my cock, my other hand sliding around the corseted curve of her waist, and she was so wet, so ready, that I didn't bother to guide myself properly to her pussy. Instead, I just shoved my hips forward as I yanked her into me, reaching up to clap my hand over her mouth right as she was about to cry out.

I felt that muffled cry against my palm, and fuck if I didn't just want to do everything I could to feel it again. With one hand still on her waist and the other over her mouth, I moved closer, pushing deeper inside, shoving through that tight wet heat until I was buried.

And then I didn't move.

"Look," I told her roughly. "Look at you. Look at where you are. Look at what you're letting me do to you."

My good girl obeyed, glancing through the crack in the curtains behind us and then turning that gaze down to where we were joined, her stare turning hot and needy as she took in the way my hips pressed into her thighs, the way her clit pressed into the hard muscle above my dick. And suddenly I knew that I could make her come just like this, without moving, without any of those finger tricks or tongue tricks I'd become so famous in certain circles for. Just by filling her, just by making her breathe and squirm around my length, by making her *feel* the hard thickness that wanted only her pussy and no one else's. And of course, whispering in her ear about all the filthy things I wanted to do to her while I had my hand over her mouth.

"I'm going to fuck your ass next," I told her. "I'm going to bury my cock so deep inside your ass that you'll forget your own name. You'll forget anything other than my dick."

Her breathing hitched, her pussy clenching around me. I smiled wickedly.

"You're so ready for me to fuck you, buttercup. Why is that? You like being fucked where anyone can see you? Or are you just so desperate for me that you'll fuck me no matter where we are?"

I pulled out slowly and watched as I did, loving the way my cock came out wet and glistening. I knew she could feel every inch of the slide, the drag of my helmeted tip as it ran along her channel. And she watched the entire process greedily, hungrily, whimpering with relief against my hand when I oh-so-slowly pushed back inside her cunt.

She tried to grind closer, to buck her hips into me, but I slid my hand from her mouth to her neck and she froze. Her eyes flashed with fear, with lust, with something deeper and more profound than both, and I drank it in as I also drank in the feeling of her pussy tight around me, the feeling of her still trying to grind into me in small movements that she hoped I wouldn't notice.

But I did notice.

"You better stay fucking still and fucking quiet," I told her, and she opened her mouth to speak—in anger or in fear, I didn't know—and then I finished my threat, "or I won't let you come."

She shut her mouth.

"Good girl. You want to come, don't you?"

She nodded frantically.

"Yeah? You like it when I make you come?"

Another nod. More squirming.

"I thought so." I gripped her neck tighter. "Stay. *Still.*"

She finally stopped trying to grind against me, but she had to squeeze her eyes shut in concentration, and the sight of it was so adorable that I dropped a kiss on each closed eyelid. "My good girl," I whispered. "Now I want you to listen to me. You feel my cock inside you? You feel how hard it is for you?"

"Yes," she murmured, eyes still closed. "I feel it."

"It's stretching your little cunt now. It's so deep inside of you that I can feel your womb. And all of it—that womb, that cunt—it belongs to me now, you understand? It belongs to me, and if I want to spread you wide and fuck you in front of everyone you know, I get to."

"Yes," she said, the word almost a moan. "You get to."

And then her eyes fluttered open. "Oh, please, Silas," she begged, and she'd gone from that petulant impatience to something more stripped and more primal. "Please make me come."

Behind us, the band struck up a new song, a popular song, and I could hear the normal ballroom chatter ripple with approval and delight. The noises seemed to blend together—the glasses clinking and the shoes thudding on the floor and the voices sharing gossip and news and advice; all of it was occasionally punctuated with a laugh or a clink that was a little too close, which made it all the more thrilling. Any moment we could be discovered, and *fuck* if a part of me didn't want that to happen.

"What would you do if someone heard you say those words?" I said harshly. My hand closed tighter around her neck. "If someone walked around this corner now and looked into the curtains? If they saw you with your legs spread wide for me?"

She made an incoherent noise. I smiled viciously at her. "You would let them watch, wouldn't you? You'd let them watch, because that's how much you need my cock. That's how much you need me. You'd let some stranger watch you getting fucked and you wouldn't care, so long as I made that pussy come for me. Isn't that right?"

"God, yes," she moaned, and it was loud enough that I glanced around behind me to see if we'd been overheard. We hadn't, at least not that I could see.

I returned my attention to her, to the way her breathing had grown labored against the squeeze of my fingers on her throat. I took care to make sure she could still breathe easily enough, but I wanted her to feel that edge of fear, that edge of uncertainty. Molly O'Flaherty had never let fear get the better of her. She'd never let fear take residence inside her mind.

Unless she was with me.

I should feel terrible about that. But I didn't. Not with that flush staining her cheeks and chest, not with the way her fingers grasped at my jacket. It occurred to me that I'd never fucked like this—only with words, only with a hand squeezing and releasing and squeezing again on her neck.

With my cock sunk to the hilt, but unmoving, a rigid bar in the soft heat of her body.

"I can do anything I want with you, can't I?" I asked her. "I can fuck you in the middle of a crowded ballroom. I can bend you over and fuck your ass until you come and cry at the same time. I can share your cunt with Castor or Julian."

Her eyes went wide at that—but not just with shock. With *lust*. I'd said it merely to be dirty, merely to drive her closer to the edge, but once I spoke the words, I felt my own response to the idea, a hot knife of arousal deep in my groin, a sharp desire that made my balls tighten. God, to see her under Castor's massive muscular frame or pinned under Julian's lean body—it was a thought that would make most men furious, but for some reason, it made me wild with desire. It made me deranged with the need to drive into her, to rut like an animal. I *wanted* to see her with my friends, I *wanted* to be the one to be able to share her.

My thighs trembled with the restraint it took to stay still. "You've gone quiet, Mary Margaret. Is it because you want to be shared? Is it because you want me to spread your legs and offer you to other lovers?"

Her mouth parted, lips berry pink and plump, and oh God, now the memories were crashing in, memories of her lips wrapped tightly around Julian's cock, of all those long nights in Europe where Julian and I each took our turn with her, making her come over and over and over again, until we all fell asleep in a pile of tangled limbs. Of the time Castor had given in to his lust and curiosity one night during supper, and Molly had—only for that one night—allowed him to dominate her right there on his dinner table. He'd laid her out and tied her down and fucked her until she screamed with an orgasm so powerful it shook the table.

Why doesn't that make you jealous? I asked myself. But it didn't make me jealous.

It only made me harder.

"Maybe I should pull out of you right now and go find Castor or Julian, hmm? Bring them back here to fuck you. I'll bring Ivy too, and maybe I'll make you watch while I sink my cock into her. Make you watch as I test her cunt to see if it's as tight and wet as yours."

Wrong words. Sinful words. Awful words.

But Molly's eyes had fluttered closed again and her breathing was so fast, so rapid now, and that flush was so deep and so hot in her skin, and she whispered, "Oh God, oh God, oh God." Her hands were fisted in my jacket, and she couldn't help the squirming, the wriggling, the need for friction.

I let her move against me as I continued. "I want to see Julian and Castor inside of you at the same time. And I want to fuck Ivy while I watch. And then, when they're done using you, I will wrap my hand in Ivy's hair—" I slid the hand from her waist up into her gorgeous mass of curls to prove my point "—and drag her over to your cunt and make her lick you until you can't speak any more."

"*Jesus Christ*," she managed, and I could tell we were there, that our fantasy had taken us there, and I finally clamped down against her airway as hard as I dared, keeping a mental clock in my mind to make sure she stayed safe. Everything about her was open, needy—her cunt and her parted mouth and her widened blue eyes—and everything about me was hard and tense and rigid.

"And then after they've all had you, after they've come in you, then I'll get you. And you'll be so sensitive and swollen, and I'll fuck you for hours, as a punishment and a reward. Look down, Molly. Look at you grinding against my cock like a needy little thing. I bet you can't wait to have all of us using you, filling you with our seed."

The first wave was more like a ripple, a small tug, and I

brutishly thrust up into it even though I was already sunk all the way in, stabbing myself into her climax as I finally let go of her neck. Air sucked into her lungs, and her orgasm doubled and tripled and quadrupled all in the few seconds it took for her to call my name.

"*Fuck*, Silas!"

She writhed and gasped, and I kept pressing into her, needing to feel every twitch and flutter and clench, needing my whole dick to feel every second of this orgasm, this first *I-choose-you* orgasm. I forced myself to stay completely still as she quivered around me, clenching my jaw with the effort of restraint as her narrow channel gripped and slid against me.

She ground against me through it all, wrapping her legs around my waist to lock us close together, the pink bud of her clit rubbing shamelessly against me.

God, I loved it. I loved *her*. And I had to start moving right the fuck now.

As the last of her climax fluttered away, leaving Molly panting and slumped against the glass behind her, I widened my legs and started driving into her pussy in earnest, loving the image of my thick cock pulling out to the tip and then ramming back in. She was so wet, so deliciously wet, but swollen, and the coupling of the lubrication and the resistance was almost too much to bear. I didn't go fast so much as I went hard, rocking her back with every thrust and making her squeak with mingled pleasure and discomfort.

With a growl, I moved her feet back to where they had been—braced against the sides of the window—so that she was wide open for me. Yes, that was good, I liked that. I liked my hands around her tiny waist, I liked her cunt open and ready, I liked the noise of the party guests and the thrill of the public event behind me.

"So fucking wet," I grunted. My balls slapped against her ass with each thrust. "So fucking wet for me."

Her flush deepened and I knew she'd come again—if I could last that long. Which was a matter for debate, at this point. "Rub your clit," I ordered her. "Rub it hard and fast. I want you to make me come when you do."

"Yes, Silas," she whispered, her hand already snaking down to find her swollen nub. I watched her slender fingers work herself, and she watched me watching her, and then she fell over the edge once more, her head falling back as she tried to hold in her cry. That's all I needed—the long arch of her throat as her head dropped back, the wet clench of her orgasm—and then I was following her over the cliff into oblivion.

The climax started deep in my body, a jagged thing sawing at the base of my spine, sawing deep into my balls and cock, and it hurt it felt so good, my whole body shrinking to one point—my cock—and then exploding outwards as I shot jet after hot jet of cum deep into her body. I held her tighter and thrust harder as that happened, wanting to fill her up with as much of me as I could. To mark her and claim her and fucking own her.

I pulsed and pulsed for what felt like hours, fucking through the climax like a man possessed, until finally the light returned to my vision and the sensation of anything beyond my orgasm began to come back. Molly's hands in my hair. The sticky warmth we'd made between us. The music still trilling in the background.

I sucked in a breath. "Jesus."

Molly gave me an exhausted, sated smile—free of all sarcasm and impatience and calculation. A smile I remembered well from those idyllic three days we'd spent together. "I know." She reached for my hand. "I know."

I slid out of her, already missing the messily perfect connection, and then squatted down again without bothering to tuck myself back inside my pants. I had to see this first, this image that I'd fantasized about for so long.

"Stay as you are," I said firmly, giving her pussy a small spank to make sure she heard me. Her thighs quivered, but she kept them spread for me.

Using my thumbs, I parted her folds; I reached for her hand and then directed her fingers to her entrance, guiding them to push inside. Slowly, deliberately, she gave me the show I wanted, the show that was getting me hard again, already. She moved her slick fingers in and out, pushing my cum farther up into herself. My dick gave a jolt as I thought about the implications of this kind of ownership, as I thought about her belly growing heavy with my child.

Is there anything better than this? Than fucking this perfect woman, than having her choose me? Than having this future where I can imagine children?

I groaned as she lifted her fingers to her mouth to suck our mingled juices off of them. "*Fuck*, Molly. You're going to kill me."

"Not if you don't fuck me to death first."

I buried my face in her neck, inhaling her cinnamon scent before pulling away. "Don't tempt me, buttercup."

CHAPTER 8

MOLLY

*S*ilas cleaned us both as best as he could with his handkerchief, and then we rearranged our clothes. I peeked out from behind the curtain, expecting maybe an enraged Hugh or a prurient spy or two, but there was no one. The guests still danced and dined and drank to celebrate a wedding that wouldn't happen.

The wedding won't happen!

That was incredible and wonderful to think. I'd decided to throw it all away when I saw Silas tonight, tall and dashing, his blue eyes sparkling with love and mischief and intelligence. But then he'd told me about what he and Julian had done, and while part of me did truly resist the notion of being rescued, the practical Molly was already adding together stakes and shares and ships and warehouses, dividing and multiplying and cataloging the infinite number of contingencies that must be planned for.

I was so incredibly grateful, and I turned to tell him that

when I realized he wasn't in the curtained alcove with me anymore. Prodding at my hair with tentative fingertips to make sure it wasn't too disheveled, I walked out of the alcove, searching for Silas.

"My Molly."

I turned, and there he was, holding a glass of cold water. I took it eagerly, heat flaring in my sensitive core as I noticed how hungrily he watched me as I drank. How hungrily he watched my throat as I swallowed.

"Are you going to tell Hugh now?" Silas asked. "Or wait until after the party?"

"I—" I wasn't sure. I had raced ahead to what this all meant for O'Flaherty Shipping and had embraced that delicious, fantastical idea of loving Silas freely, but I hadn't yet thought pragmatically about breaking off my engagement. Or indeed, even entering into a new one with Silas.

A new engagement. Another sudden marriage. Are you really ready for that?

The thoughts thudded into me like anchors dropping into the sea—heavy and dragging and nearly impossible to reel back in once they'd been cast out. I loved Silas, I wanted to be with him, I knew these things…so then why was the idea of chaining myself to another man so terrifying? Why, when it was the man I wanted to be chained to, the man I'd been willing to abandon my company for just half an hour ago?

But it was terrifying. So terrifying that I had to turn away from him, masking my discomfiture by taking another drink of water.

"You don't have to tell him tonight," Silas said gently, circling around me so we faced each other once again. I kept my eyes past his shoulder, watching the dancers twirl in a carefree waltz. "But the sooner you tell him, the sooner we can announce our own engagement."

Another drink. Another moment staring at the dancers.

"Molly?" Silas prompted, his voice worried. He ducked down to meet my eyes. "Is everything okay? Are you—" horror flooded his features "—I didn't hurt you just now, did I? I didn't make you do anything you didn't want to do?"

I sighed. "Of course not. I have a safe word, don't I? You trust me to say it when something is too much and I'll trust you to stop when I say it. Agreed?"

"Agreed," he said, his eyes still trained on mine. "But then what is it? You seem...distant...all of a sudden."

"It's just..." *Don't say it, Molly. Whatever you're feeling is just the temporary natural reaction to all of these sudden changes, and saying it will only hurt him pointlessly.*

But there he was with those blue eyes so sweet and that face so hopeful and loving and open, and I didn't want to start this new phase of our lives with a lie designed to spare his feelings while suppressing my own. I wanted honesty and openness, and most of all, I wanted to know that he would still love me even when I was being complicated and difficult.

"Do we have to get engaged so soon?" I asked finally, the words coming out in a rush. "I mean, it will take time for the word to spread about Hugh and me, and the damage to our reputations if we have a rushed engagement..."

Silas frowned, his eyebrows pulling together in the most adorable way. "I care about your reputation, Molly, but in the past, our circle...We don't care about reputations."

"We do if it will harm the company."

"Molly, is there anything that can harm the company's reputation more than what Cunningham has done?"

I scrambled for another excuse, another reason to delay the engagement, but I couldn't find anything. Because there was nothing, other than my strange, sudden panic that I was casting myself back into the fire after Silas's financial maneuvering had offered me a way out.

The light had dimmed in Silas's eyes and his eyebrows un-furrowed. "You don't want to marry me," he said flatly. "Is that what it is?"

"No!" I responded quickly. "I do! I do want to be with you. It's just—you and Julian have made it so I don't *have* to marry anyone. Is it so terrible just to enjoy that fact for a while? That I can choose someone of my own free will, at whatever time I want?"

Silas licked his lips, an unconscious habit he had while he thought. My body came alive at the sight of that tongue and the memories it evoked, but I forced my constant need for Silas aside.

"Please," I begged him. "I love you. But I want some time before I resign myself to marriage again."

"*Resign yourself to marriage?*" he repeated incredulously. "Do you even hear yourself? You sound absurd. Marriage between two people that love each other isn't meant to be servitude. It's supposed to be joyful and fulfilling."

"And I know it would be that with you," I reassured. "It's just that I will be ending one engagement tonight, and I am not ready to plunge into another. Not without some time for reflection. I mean, we have all the time in the world, Silas. We love each other. There's no need to rush into marriage."

He didn't answer right away, but then he took a step closer to me, his hand cupping the back of my elbow. It was a gesture that looked polite and seemly from a distance, but that felt possessive and stern and intimate up close. "Do you remember my demand when I asked you to marry me last month?"

I remembered. The Baron's party. The small private corner we'd found. My pussy riding Silas's fingers after he coaxed a world-shattering climax out of me.

"You asked me for a baby," I said.

"And I meant it. Molly, I want a family. I want a family

84

with you. I want your belly full of my children. And I want it as soon as possible. Yes, that sounds possessive and boorish, and I can't explain it in a way that isn't so aggressively male, but I love you so much and I can't imagine having a family that you're not a part of."

His words melted me, tugged at me, made me angry with myself for this inexcusable and unanticipated ambivalence. And he was right to want to start a family soon; I was nearly thirty years old and having children was something that shouldn't be waited on much longer. But I couldn't just wish this reluctance away. It came from a place that wasn't rational or logical. It came from a place of deep fear.

"Just give me a day," I said. "One day. To end things with Hugh and to think. It's all too much right now."

Silas wasn't the type to storm off. He wasn't the type to fight. He was the type to smile and joke and embrace, until the conflict melted away in the face of his sheer resolve to fill his sphere with affection and light.

But there were no smiles or embraces for me right now. Instead, he took my hand and kissed it, and said, "Then I shall see you tomorrow night," in a cold voice that betrayed how hurt he was.

And then he was gone.

⁓

SILAS

How had I gone from one of the most intense orgasms I'd ever had to abandoning Molly on the ballroom floor? She'd looked so lost and so confused, and yet so determined, and I loved her so much, but I was also furious with her. Hurt by her.

After all we'd been through, after all I'd done for her, after all her noble words about sacrificing everything to be with me—she was scared of actually marrying me? Part of me knew it must be her independence dictating this fear, her need for autonomy and freedom, but what if it was actually because I'd been too rough with her during sex? Or too demanding with my desire for a family?

Or—and I knew this thought came from a dark, ridiculous place, but I couldn't ignore it—what if it was because she loved me less now? That she didn't have to marry Hugh to save her company? Maybe I had been the attractive forbidden option, but now that I was no longer forbidden and she was free of any obligation to marry, she'd realized she didn't want me?

In a terrible mood—made more terrible by the fact that such moods were usually alien to me—I stomped out of my carriage and stomped into my townhouse, throwing my jacket and hat onto the floor, slamming doors, and growling at any servant that came near me. How could they understand? How could they possibly help?

No. Only gin could help me now.

I went into the parlor and poured myself a stiff glass, and right as I was about to take my first much-needed drink, a banging sounded at the door.

Molly.

At this hour, it could only be Molly. To apologize, to rail at me, I suddenly didn't care. I needed to see her. I needed answers and reassurance and the smell and feel of her against me. I suddenly needed to know that she still loved me. No, more than that. I needed to know that she loved me as much as I loved her. Because I couldn't bear the lonely reality of being the one who cared the most.

I couldn't.

But when I flung open the door, it wasn't Molly I saw but a solemn-looking young man—illuminated in the dim gaslights along the street—extending a small envelope. It took my tired, emotional mind several seconds to process the scene, but once I did, I knew it would stay with me forever: the anonymous delivery boy, the London fog swirling behind him, the innocuous-looking envelope that would change my life.

"Thank you," I said, fishing a coin from somewhere to tip him. I took the envelope and closed the door.

It was strange to get a telegram so late, and somehow I knew, though I couldn't explain how, that it portended bad news. It was the lateness of the hour or the solemnity of the delivery boy or maybe even the heavy fog outside, that fog that crept up from the river at night, as if to remind us glitzy, happy Londoners that sterner, ancient powers still held sway over our lives.

Or maybe it was the origin of the message smudgily printed on the back in hasty ink.

Vaison-la-Romaine.

The closest town to Thomas and Charlotte's villa in Provence. The closest telegraph station to the house that held, aside from Molly and Julian and Castor, the dearest people in the world to me.

I tore open the envelope right there by the door, my hands shaking and my heart thumping with dread, and when I read the contents inside, I sank down to the floor, where I buried my face in my hands and cried.

CHAPTER 9

MOLLY

I hated myself a little.

Well, not a little. A lot. I hated myself a lot. And the steel fortitude it took to go back into the bustle of the party and smile and shake hands was indescribable. I simpered and smiled, all with tears burning my eyes and Silas's seed still damp between my legs, all with this leaden ball of self-hatred and confusion hanging from my heart, and somehow, *barely*, I managed to keep my voice even and my face clear for the rest of the night.

Even as I felt waves of panic about marrying Silas.

Even as my body still tingled and buzzed with the memory of his touch.

It was so stupid—really, quite idiotic—that this panic would come, so unexpectedly and so inconveniently, when for the last month, I'd known in my heart that Silas was the one man I could be happy marrying. That Silas was the one man I wanted to be with.

But surely he understood? That this whole idea of marrying for my company had been thrust upon me without my consent? That I hadn't necessarily been ready for it before it became the economically expedient thing for me to do?

If only he would give me time to think about it and explain. Because it wasn't that I didn't love him—I loved him so intensely it frightened me. It was more that I wanted to make sure when we moved forward together, we did it on my terms—on even footing, as it were. Not while I was still reeling from this horrible situation and all of the horrible demands it'd tried to place on me.

That was fair, right? To want an engagement to come from a place of serenity and joy? And not simply dazed relief?

The party went late, the music and drinks and colloquy lasting until the clock struck four, and then finally, the last of our guests filtered sleepily out of the rented hall, leaving Hugh and me alone. He turned to me, offering his elbow to escort me down to our carriage, and for a moment, I saw him as he was when we'd first met, seven or eight years ago. Hopeful and arrogant and a little lost—the kind of handsome man who'd been able to drift along the river of society without any effort. I think maybe I'd seen something endearing in that privileged innocence, that cloistered experience. Maybe I'd seen myself as I wanted to be—untouched by cynicism and violence. Carefree and careless. Because, while I'd maybe appeared carefree to an outsider, it was a constant, conscious, and exhausting act. But Hugh—his easiness was real and unfeigned, and maybe like Polidori's vampire, I'd imagined I could somehow siphon that from him and infuse my own life with that kind of blithe insouciance.

Of course, I knew better now. And I knew that Hugh

lacked certain qualities that his untroubled comportment couldn't make up for. He wasn't witty or charming, like Silas, or magnetic and secretly dominant, like Silas, or tender and perceptive...like Silas.

He wasn't Silas, and he never would be, and the fact that I had ever imagined a marriage to Hugh would be anything less than torture was supremely laughable now.

The words poured out easily. I put my hand over Hugh's and looked him in the eye. "I'm ending our engagement."

Hugh's surprised laugh echoed through the empty ball-room, a laugh that said *good joke, Molly, so hilarious*. Irritation flamed at that, but I pushed it down, along with the urge to feel the crack of my hand against his cheek.

"I'm serious, Hugh."

His laughter died. "Dearest, what can you possibly mean? You know that you—"

"—have to marry you to keep my company intact?" I finished for him. "Maybe. Maybe this is the end of O'Flaherty Shipping. But I realized tonight that there's nothing worth the price of my happiness. That my father wouldn't want this for me, even to save the company he built. I'm sorry, Hugh, but I'm walking away from our agreement."

His brown eyes blinked—confused and a little desperate as things began to sink in. "Molly, you cannot be serious. We just hosted almost every worthy member of London society for our engagement ball, and you want to tell me that you've changed your mind? It's too late!"

I removed my arm from his, taking a step back. "Legally and practically, no, Hugh. It's not too late. I'm sorry that this will be socially embarrassing for you, but really, can it be more embarrassing than your own cousin standing trial for seducing a girl of barely sixteen years?"

He gaped at me.

"Face it. Without Cunningham's money and without my

company, you're essentially finished. And with two scandals under your belt in less than a month, well, good luck finding a wealthy bride willing to marry you. I liked you once, and you know, I still believe that you do sincerely like me, in your own way. But that's not enough to make up for a loveless union. Especially the kind of union that you wanted with me, where I would have been trapped and isolated, without any recourse."

"No," he rushed in to say. "It doesn't have to be that way. We can edit those contracts, Molly. We can fix things."

It was almost sweet he thought that would be enough to lure me into staying. I patted his shoulder. "Goodbye, Hugh. My solicitors will be in touch."

I FOUGHT the urge to go to Silas right away. Rather, I went home and bathed, slipping into bed as the sun began blooming pink and orange on the horizon. I tried not to think about what I'd just done—alienating Silas and breaking things off with Hugh. I tried not to think about whether or not I would have this house in a year, whether or not I'd be able to afford my servants and my carriage and to feed myself.

I simply closed my eyes and remembered the precise shade of blue Silas's eyes were when he came inside of me, when he'd muttered *Jesus*, as if I were the holiest thing next to God that he could think of.

He would understand once I explained it all to him properly. He would understand how deeply I needed him, and how deeply I needed his patience. I knew he would.

When I woke several hours later, I felt groggy and shameful somehow, as if sleeping late were a sin. The afternoon sunlight spilled into the room, and there was a warm cup of tea beside me—evidence that breakfast had been brought in and then taken back, and probably the same with lunch, and now it was past time for both.

I struggled to sit up, feeling a delicious soreness in my cunt as I did, and for a moment forgetting all the complicated pain of last night. All I remembered was the feeling of Silas's fingers digging into my waist and throat, the filthy words he'd crooned in my ear as I'd writhed with that insane orgasm.

And then it all came back. Our fight. His cold voice and the even colder kiss to the back of my hand.

The fragile sense of hope I'd tried to cultivate as I'd fallen asleep had vanished somewhere along the way, like mist burned off by the afternoon sunlight. I felt only remorse and defensiveness and the grim fear that I may have ruined the most important thing that would ever happen to me in my life.

I have to see him. Now.

I threw off the covers and rang the bell for my lady's maid, and within an hour, I was clad in a white and green day dress, a fashionable hat pinned into my hair, and delicate white gloves covering my fingers. I rubbed at the spot where my engagement ring had been as the carriage jolted and jerked through the afternoon clog of London's busiest streets.

And then we were there, and I was flinging open the door to the carriage even before it had completely stopped, tripping down the carriage steps and rushing up the stairs to knock at the door.

What should I say? What words would expose everything I needed him to see—my love and my fear, and most of all, my need for him to understand me?

Or maybe it shouldn't be words. Silas and I had always been physical, always been creatures of touch and desire.

Maybe I would say nothing as I approached him. Maybe I would slide his jacket off his shoulders and tear at his cravat. Maybe I'd push him down onto his sofa and bounce on his cock until we were both covered in sweat and sin.

Just the thought of doing that made me shiver with anticipation and desire, made my nipples hard and tight against the constricting press of my corset. *Yes. That's what I'll do.*

But when the door opened, it was Silas's butler, already bowing and intoning something in his low, clipped voice.

"Pardon?" I asked.

"Mr. Cecil-Coke is not present today. Nor will he be home at any time in the foreseeable future. I'm afraid that he's left London in order to tend to a personal matter."

Not home.

Left London.

Personal matter.

"Can you be any more specific?" I asked desperately. "It really is urgent that I speak to him right away."

"I'm sorry," the butler said firmly and a little disapprovingly. "I'm not at liberty to divulge anything more. If you'd like, I can send word that you've called."

"I—yes. All right." I fumbled for one of my cards in my purse and handed it to the servant. "Please let him know that I've come to visit. And is there any place where I can forward a letter to?"

Perhaps I looked frantic enough or perhaps he simply wanted me to leave, because he sighed and relented. "Vaison-La-Romaine in Provence would be the place, miss. Now if you'll excuse me…"

I nodded numbly, stepping back so he could shut the door, trying to wrap my mind around this new information.

Provence.

Silas had left for France.

But why? To see his brother and sister-in-law at their rented villa like he had last year? To lick his wounds?

Was it a move calculated out of hurt...or out of anger?

Stunned, I made my way back to the carriage, my mind turning the entire ride home. That the selfish bastard had left right after this fight without a single word—without even a hastily jotted note—what kind of callous cruelty had been driving him?

I rested my head against the side of the carriage and pressed my eyes shut, trying to keep the blossoming tears at bay.

SILAS

There was no grave in Provence, no long mound of humped, rich earth. For a long, terrible moment, I felt a homesickness for England so strong it nearly brought me to my knees. That I should miss something as somber and gloomy as a graveyard—me, Silas, the smiling prankster at every party— would have seemed ridiculous not four days ago. But, none-theless. I missed the deep green of English graveyard grass, the aged dignity of the weathered stones. Instead, Charlotte and her unborn child were deposited in a cramped forest of sandstone crypts and vaults, a miniature city of the dead, ceaselessly swept by the hot lavender-scented wind.

She should be buried at home, I thought distantly as the wind ruffled the flowers little Henry had placed on top of her crypt. An English grave for one of the best and loveliest Englishwomen I'd ever known.

But there had been no time. The warm Provencal climate had dictated the practical necessities, and with Thomas currently hovering in a state of near-death himself, there'd been no one other than the town officials to make the decision. Charlotte Cecil-Coke, mother of five and pregnant with the unborn sixth, had died of cholera four days past and had been interred in the nearest Protestant cemetery the day before I'd arrived.

I'd brought the children—even tiny Silas, still less than a year old—to see their mother's grave. Partly because I knew they needed this moment, however hard and however sad, because I'd needed it when my own mother and father had died. That moment of standing in the graveyard and hearing nothing except the wind and the rustle of moving grass and the sounds of distant birds and insects, and *knowing*, knowing deep in your heart, that no other noise would come. That the silence was eternal now that our loved ones had finally passed away, and that our pain was the price of their newfound peace.

And partly, because back at the villa, their father was enduring unbearable and exhausting agony, and though I wanted them to be able to say goodbye, I also wanted to shield them from the worst of his suffering. Luckily, their nanny—a sturdy Welsh widow who'd been with them for more than a year—was here to help, even though I think she cried louder than any of the children as she laid her own flowers on Charlotte's grave.

Me, I cried silently the whole time we were there. Hugging Albert, who at nine, was trying his best to be manly and stoic. Holding Jane and Henry's hands—who as the next eldest understood that their momma was never coming back. And then cradling Aurora and Silas at turns, both of whom were too young to grasp the pain of the moment.

I cried for Charlotte. I cried for the children, and for the little baby who I'd never get to meet. And most of all, I cried for Thomas. For the one goodbye I had never been prepared to face.

That night, after Bertha and I had put the sober, stunned children to bed, I went to Thomas, who like last night when I'd arrived, was sleeping.

Sweat clung to his pale skin and dark circles shadowed his eyes. A local woman had been hired to nurse him, and I sat by his bed and watched as she carefully sponged his face and adjusted his blankets. I knew that he'd been vomiting constantly since he'd contracted the illness, and a detached part of me was impressed with how clean she'd kept the bed and Thomas's person. No doubt it was her assiduous care and attention that had kept him hanging on for this many days when it had taken Charlotte so quickly.

"The physician said most likely tonight or tomorrow," she told me quietly in French as she built up the fire. "We can call him at any time to administer more opium, if your brother seems to be in a lot of discomfort."

"*Merci*," I said woodenly. I *was* grateful, for all of the kindness these strangers had shown my brother's family in my absence. But the feeling was so small compared to the vast emptiness that yawned over the next sunrise. In a matter of hours, my brother would be dead. The man I loved and looked up to, the man I wanted to become like as I grew older. And no other thought could outweigh that. There was no distraction. No hope.

Only the heavy, all-consuming fog of imminent death.

I stared at Thomas's handsome and drawn face, at the labored and shallow movements of his chest as he struggled to breathe. And then darkness crept into the sides of my vision as sleep mercifully claimed me.

According to the clock on the mantel, it was almost dawn when I jerked awake, my neck stiff and sore from sleeping in a chair. I rolled my head from side to side, thinking about calling the nurse in, when I noticed Thomas looking at me with half-closed lids. His eyes—a heterochromatic blend of amber and blue and green that had always made the girls around the manor swoon when we were boys—were tired and bloodshot and sunken. But they were alert, and his mouth pulled into a smile when he saw that I was awake.

"Silas," he croaked, and I pulled my chair closer.

"Don't try to speak," I said gently. "The doctor said you should save your strength."

"For what?" he said hoarsely. "It hardly takes strength to die."

I thought I was prepared for this, or at the very least, beginning to be prepared, but the bleak candor of his words felt like a punch to the throat. How could anyone ever be ready for losing someone they loved? And how could God ask someone to be cognizant of their own imminent death, as Thomas was of his own?

"Don't make that face at me," Thomas said, trying to sound teasing, but sounding only weary instead. "It's going to be fine."

"It's not going to be fine," I said, swiping at my eyes in a vain effort to contain my tears. I'd cried far too much in the last few days, and only a selfish prick would force a dying person to endure the burden of someone else's sorrow.

"It is," Thomas said, a thready confidence woven in his words. "I will get to be with my Charlotte again. And you will be an excellent father to my kids."

There was no hope of holding the tears back now. Instead, I laid my arms on the bed next to him and buried my face so that he couldn't see me sob.

"You will…you will take them, right?" The uncertainty and worry in Thomas's voice was possibly the most tragic thing I'd ever heard.

I raised my head, not bothering to wipe away the tears this time. "Of course, Thomas. I already love them as if they were my own! But you—*you* are their father. I want them to have you. *I* want to have you. Who's going to tell me what to do if you go? Who's going to give me advice and then forgive me when I ignore it?"

Thomas gave me the ghost of a smile. "I got a letter," he said, his eyes a little unfocused, and my heart dropped as I wondered if the sudden change of subject had something to do with his declining health, a loss of mental acuity, perhaps. But then he tilted his head to me, and said, "From Julian. He told me about Molly."

Molly.

"She'll take care of you," Thomas murmured. "Like Charlotte took care of me. She'll give you advice just like I did, but you won't ignore it when it comes from her."

"No, I suppose I wouldn't." A bitter lump formed in my throat. In the last few days, the ceaseless chores that had accompanied the family tragedy had kept me from dwelling on the strained way Molly and I had left things, but now that Thomas had brought her up, I felt another layer of anxious grief settle on top of what I already felt. "We didn't leave things well," I said hesitantly, not wanting to derail Thomas's hopes for me on his deathbed...but also unwilling to lie to him or myself about what the future might hold.

"What happened?" Thomas rasped.

"We can't talk about this, not now," I protested. "We can't talk about my romantic life when we should be—"

"Should be what?" Thomas interrupted weakly. "Sharing our most profound truths and long-held secrets?"

I couldn't help but laugh a little through my tears. "Yes. I thought that's what you did. When, you know."

"Someone is dying?" Thomas offered. He was so unflinching about this, so equanimous in the face of death, that I promised myself right then and there that I would be like this on my own deathbed. That I would somehow cultivate the serenity he exuded right now, even though I knew he had be wrestling with pain and exhaustion.

"Yes, when someone is dying," I conceded. And then after a moment of internal debate, I decided to tell him. The entire story, from last year up until a few days again, from love to heartbreak and then love to heartbreak once more, and he listened to the whole melodramatic saga, sometimes closing his eyes, but the small noises he made in response to my story assured me that he was indeed conscious.

"And then she asked me for a day to figure things out. Which is so painful, because I've known that she's the only person I'll ever want to marry for a year, and if she doesn't know that about me, does that mean that she loves me less than I love her? Or that she'll always love her freedom more?"

Thomas made a noise that sounded suspiciously like a derisive snort.

I narrowed my eyes. "I don't care if you're dying, I will still fight you."

That earned something like a real laugh from Thomas, although it was short-lived as the action seemed to bring on an intense wave of dizziness. He closed his eyes, and I noticed once again how ashen his face was, how hollow his features. Pain scissored across my heart.

"The real question," he whispered, his eyes still closed, "is whether you love her enough to stay with her on her terms. If you love her enough to give her whatever space and time she needs, even if she needs it until the end of your lives."

He opened his multi-colored eyes again, meeting my gaze with the full force of thirty-some years of fraternal affection. "Silas, what is more important to you? Molly? Or your pride?"

CHAPTER 10

SILAS

*T*homas died peacefully seven hours later, after getting to see his children one last time. The physician had the children don masks and stand against the far side of the wall, and so their goodbyes came in the form of stilted words from the older ones and confused tears from the youngest.

I hated that. I wanted them to hug him and kiss him. I wanted him, one last time, to have his bed invaded by a herd of snuggling, warm, wriggling kids. But in the end, it was me who invaded his bed after the children had left, remembering my own childhood and all the nights I had crawled into his bed after a bad dream. On those nights, with my older brother's sensible intonations that dreams weren't real (and also with the lamp he'd considerately light for me,) I'd fall back asleep, feeling safe and certain in the knowledge that nightmares couldn't follow me into real life. Not with Thomas beside me.

Except for today. Except for right now.

With the Occitan sun pouring in through the window, with the sounds of the baby squealing happily elsewhere in the villa, my nightmares became living, present entities. There was no escape from Thomas's labored breathing, no escape from the strange groans and wheezes he made as his body struggled valiantly against the inevitable.

He couldn't talk any more, he could barely open his eyes, and so I talked for both of us, laying on my back next to him and staring at the ceiling. I talked about Coke Manor and the parents we'd both loved so dearly. I talked about the children, and the way my heart twisted whenever I thought of Molly. And every now and again, his eyes would open or his mouth would move in the facsimile of a smile, and I knew that he was hearing me, that this in some way was soothing, my voice a constant reminder that he wasn't alone. Like he had done for me when we were children, I ushered him into sleep and darkness, and the moment that he'd finally gone, I felt it. A feeling like a hovering presence, a weight that wasn't oppressive but that nonetheless felt strange and unnatural, and then it was gone.

The room was empty—save for me—Thomas had gone from *Thomas* to *Thomas's body*, and after several long moments of numbness, I left the room to go tell his children —who were, in a sense, now my own.

A WEEK PASSED. It felt like a year and it felt like a day, and thank God for Bertha and the servants, who kept us fed and clean while I dazedly arranged for the burial. After Thomas was interred next to Charlotte, I held off making any official plans about returning to England. Instead, I sunk myself into the minute-by-minute life of my nieces and nephews, reading stories and playing chase and picking lavender alongside the road. It was an opiate, a salve, although the moment my mind opened up to the fact that this was now my life forever, my chest grew tight as I remembered why. Remembered those two sandstone crypts on that dusty hill.

The other danger of long hours of play or wandering and picking plants was that my mind also had time to drift to Molly O'Flaherty. To her hair and her smooth, freckled stomach and her shaking voice as she'd asked me for time to think.

Where was she now? Was she thinking about me, missing me, or was she simply grateful to have space away from me? She hadn't written or sent any word, although I'd been here less than two weeks, and it often took longer for letters to make their way down from England.

You should write to her.

But though I thought this more than once, I never did. Or I should say, I never finished the letter, because once I had sat down to write, I couldn't stop. I wrote pages and pages of rambling thoughts and feelings and memories, some of her and of us, and others of the brother and sister-in-law I'd just lost, and whenever I set down my pen and looked over what I had written, I knew it was an un-sendable missive. It was honest and raw and jagged and far too emotive for someone as closed off as Molly.

And then I would look around the dinner table, at the four children chattering and eating and little Silas in my lap messily squashing peas in his fist, and I would want to laugh a terrible, mirthless laugh. Molly had been afraid of getting engaged. How much more would she despise a connection with me when it came along with five children?

I remembered Thomas's words the night before he died, when he'd asked me what was more important, being with

Molly or my pride, and perhaps in another life, I would have been able to swallow my pride and open myself to being with Molly however she wanted me.

No. There was no perhaps. I would've. Because I loved her so desperately that I would take her any way I could have her.

But things were different now. I couldn't marry someone who wasn't willing to be an adoptive mother to my nieces and nephews, but also how could I ask that of any woman, much less one as skittish about commitment as Molly was?

I needed to resign myself to my new life. I would have these children who I loved like my own, but that would be it. Because Molly wouldn't take me now, and there was no other woman I would ever want other than Molly.

And the letter grew longer. And remained unsent.

MOLLY

Paris was thankfully cool on the morning I boarded the train south. The journey from London to Dover, then Dover to Calais, and then Calais to Paris, had been delayed by several days of torrential rain, which made the Channel nigh impassable and the country roads wet quagmires that sucked coach wheels deep into the muck and refused to let go. But today had—finally—dawned clear and dry, if slightly chilly, and the passage south was smooth and untroubled.

Not at all like my jumbled, fevered mind.

When I'd left Silas's house that day, hurt that he'd left without thinking to leave me so much as a note, I'd initially set down to write him, to try to explain the myriad of conflicting feelings I felt, to convey the deep, needy love I had for him and also my burning desire to be my own woman.

But as I had tried to write it, I couldn't articulate what I needed to say. Maybe it was because I wasn't sure myself what I meant. Maybe it was because I had to see his face as I explained to him, I had to know that he understood.

Or maybe it was because I already missed him so much, after only one day without him, that writing a letter felt like a painfully hollow exercise. It was no substitute for what I wanted, what I needed.

How funny that we'd spent so much of our time this last year apart, but now that everything with my aborted marriage was settled, I couldn't bear to spend another moment without him. Even though I'd told him I wasn't ready for an engagement.

What is wrong with me? I sounded utterly senseless with my inconsistent and plaintive wailings, a disconsolate child that refused to be placated by any alternative.

So after a long, lonely night, my dreams full of Silas, I had made up my mind. I would follow him to his brother's villa. If nothing else, it would show him that I *did* love him and I *did* need him. I went to my solicitor's to inform him of the termination of my engagement with Hugh, which he'd already heard about. And he'd delivered some good news, at least.

"Not all of the board members are walking away," he'd said with a smile. "A few of Cunningham's closest are. But several of them are much more hesitant to resort to something so extreme, especially since Cunningham's scandal has weakened whatever loyalty they may have had for him. And," my solicitor had added with a smile, "Martjin van der Sant sent over a business contract late last night."

"What?" I'd asked. Van der Sant had been so far out of my thoughts in the past twenty-four hours that it took me a moment to process what my solicitor was saying. "He's still going to partner with my company?"

"There was a short note attached...apparently he was quite impressed by the personal fortitude you exhibited in protecting his daughter, even knowing that it would threaten your prospects."

Birgit. While I didn't doubt that he would have come to this conclusion on his own, I also suspected that his daughter had something to do with this.

So I'd signed the papers, sending a silent *thank you* to Birgit, feeling a fledgling hope about O'Flaherty Shipping, which would have a difficult winter, perhaps, but it would survive.

It would survive.

But hope had long since given way to fretful misery as I made my way down to Provence. What did it matter if my company survived if Silas didn't want to be with me? What if the *personal matter* was just a convenient excuse he'd directed his butler to give me, and this was actually him trying to run away?

What if I got to the villa and he shut the door in my face?

It took three days for me to make it from Paris to Vaison-La-Romaine. Three agonizing days. And when I reached the hotel I'd planned on staying in, I went straight to the clerk while my things were unloaded.

"Could you tell me if there is a villa nearby rented by an English family?" I inquired in French. "Cecil-Coke would be the last name."

The clerk responded in a French that was heavy with the southern accent of the Languedoc, and I struggled to parse out his words. "There is an English family nearby," he affirmed, "though the gentleman there just died, I'm afraid. Cholera."

My heart plummeted down to my feet even as my head raced to catch up. "A gentleman died? When?"

"It's been over a week now." The clerk thought for a moment, oblivious to my quiet panic, oblivious to the cacophony inside my head.

No. It couldn't be Silas, he was so healthy when you saw him last.

But the timing's right. And cholera works fast.

No. It can't be him.

"And the gentleman's wife died too," the clerk finally said. "Before him. Fortunately, the children are all safe."

God be praised! It's not Silas!

I hated myself for the sigh of relief I heaved, because the moment I realized that it was Thomas and Charlotte who had died and that my Silas was safe, I also realized how crushed Silas would be by his brother's death.

A personal matter.

That must have been why he rushed off without a word. Not because he was angry or hurt—though he may have also been those things—but because his world was ending hundreds of miles away. His world and the world of—how many nieces and nephews did he have? Four? Five?

Guilt crashed into me. This entire time, I'd perceived this as either an act of emotional self-preservation or, worse, an act designed to deliberately hurt me. And all along, he'd been wrapped in grief, wrapped in the grief of those small orphaned children, and *Jesus*, this made every sleepless night and lonely morning feel so fucking trivial. What were a few stray tears in comparison to this kind of loss? What was the pain of a shattered romance in comparison to the pain of a dead brother?

As easy as it was to pretend when we were together, the world didn't revolve around us. The world was cruel and harsh and full of unexpected pain, and it had yanked Silas away without a care for my needs or even his. And I had been so petty and shallow and selfish to have never even considered that Silas's trip had nothing to do with me.

I suddenly felt very small. And very stupid.

I arranged for a carriage up to the villa, my mind churning the entire time. It was as if I were King Lear, only too late realizing my destructive self-absorption and narrowness of my vision, and like Lear, I was close to madness and weeping. I'd been so focused on my company and on me, and how could I not see that Silas was the only thing that made me happy? The only person who completed me?

Why had I run away from my own happiness?

Twilight had set around the villa, pale crepuscular light casting long shadows around the walls and tiled roof, clustering in between the even rows of fading autumn lavender stretching out toward the horizon. I walked through these shadows after exiting my carriage, flexing my fingers and reminding myself to breathe.

Breathe breathe breathe.

Because Silas had every right to shut me out of his grief. He had every right to turn me away, even if his brother hadn't died, because of how we'd left things.

I prayed that he wouldn't, though. I prayed that he'd unleash his anger and his hurt on me, punish me and use me, make me suffer as he used my body to soothe the ache inside him—anything but shut me out.

Voices spilled out of the courtyard as I approached, happy voices. The heavy wooden doors were cracked, and so I could see the scene inside, lit by several hanging lanterns, and when I saw it, my throat closed with emotion.

There he was, my Silas, tall and handsome and already a little tanned from his two weeks here in France. He was dressed more casually than he hardly ever was—trousers and a white shirt with sleeves rolled up to the elbow. A tie loosely knotted around his neck, loose enough to expose the dip of his collarbone and the jut of his Adam's apple. A day-old beard roughened those sharp cheekbones and that even sharper jaw, and in the lantern-light, his blue eyes looked deep purple or black. He was laughing—an infectiously happy sound that resounded in my very bones—and my chest tightened as I realized that was so quintessentially Silas. Laughing in the face of tragedy. Finding joy in pain.

He was chasing four small children, his laughs interspersed with chesty mock-growls, and his loping gait punctuated by low, long swipes of his arms. He was clearly supposed to a bear of some sort, and the children squealed with fearful delight when he drew close enough seize them, which he did often and then tickled them until they begged for mercy.

And in the corner, sitting on a chair, a stout older woman dandied a baby on her knee, and Silas would also occasionally stop to plant a kiss on the little one's head with a gentle affection.

If the mere act of witnessing a scene such as this had the power to impregnate, then I would be pregnant this instant. Watching Silas in his element, with the people he cared about, made my face flush with happiness. Not the selfish kind of happiness I was used to, but that almost spiritual kind of happiness that you feel in response to someone else's. I was happy that Silas was happy, regardless of the fact that I wasn't currently part of that happiness.

But the thought came anyway. *You don't belong here.*

And I didn't. I was intruding. Silas had created a small island of joy for his family in the midst of all this pain, and who was I to invade that with my need to apologize? My need for resolution?

I would come back, I decided. Later maybe. Or I could send a letter...yes, that would be best. A short letter or an invitation to talk. That would be the polite thing to do, given the circumstances.

I turned, moving away from the courtyard door and back to my waiting carriage, and then I heard his voice.

"Molly?"

CHAPTER 11

SILAS

*T*here was a pause between my saying her name and her turning back, and for a brief instant, I wondered if I'd imagined her face at the courtyard door, imagined the lantern-light glinting in her copper hair.

But then she turned and, after a moment's hesitation, stepped through the door, her figure resolving itself out of the shadows. She was real.

She was *here*.

My Molly.

Something was swelling in my chest, something heavy and light all at the same time, and it took me a moment to recognize the feeling of simple, pure happiness. Thomas had only been dead a week, and the feeling was already so foreign and strange, as if it had been years since I'd felt it instead of days.

She'd obviously been traveling all day; her fashionably striped silk dress was noticeably creased and her hair was slightly tousled from the wind. But she looked more beautiful than she'd ever looked to me, set against the Provençal dusk, her normally fierce face shy and vulnerable as my nieces and nephews rushed up to her to ask her who she was, where she was from, if she had any sweets.

And when she bent down to say hello, her rumpled hair spilling over her shoulder and creating a swinging shadow on the swan-like curve of her neck, something other than my heart started swelling too. *Fuck.* That neck and that hair. How had I forgotten how painfully sexy she was? How irresistible? How effortlessly destructive she could be with just a casual flick of her hair or a smiling one-shouldered shrug?

Collecting myself—and discreetly adjusting myself—I stepped forward to rescue her from the herd of children.

"Come inside," I said, offering a hand to her.

She slid her slender fingers into mine, her eyes raising up, sapphires framed in dark ruby lashes. The hollows and curves of her face were filled with shadows, and she looked sadder and wiser than when I'd last seen her.

"I don't want to intrude," she whispered.

"Please, Mary Margaret."

She flushed, a flush that was barely visible right now, but that I knew would stain her chest as well as her cheeks. Perhaps she was remembering all the times I'd used her name as I'd fucked her, as I'd held her down and made her come again and again for me.

And now I was remembering too.

I angled my body away from the others in the courtyard and leaned in. "Either you can walk inside yourself or I can throw you over my shoulder and carry you in—and then spank you later for your impertinence. What is it going to be?"

Her eyes grew round and her lips parted. "Both options are tempting," she breathed.

"Naughty girl."

I tugged on her hand, and together we walked inside the house.

BERTHA and I put the children to bed, and then I sent someone down to the kitchen to bring up a supper for Molly, since I guessed she hadn't eaten. Rather than eat in the dining hall with its vast dining table and cavernous ceilings, I had her installed on the villa's portico, which overlooked the lavender fields, lush carpets in the night.

The sky was a breathtaking dome of twinkling stars; the Milky Way wreathed purple and pink-gold directly in front of us. Molly had her face tilted up to the sky, eyes pinned to the colorful display as if searching for meaning there.

"*La Voie Lactée*," I murmured, setting down a silver tray of food and wine.

She smiled, keeping her eyes on the sky. "Even in French, it sounds so domestic. *The Milky Way*. Such a humble name for such incredible beauty."

I gazed at her, drinking her in. "That happens sometimes, Molly."

"Are you saying my name is humble?" she asked, not missing a beat.

"I would never."

With a sigh, she finally tore her eyes away from the stars and looked to me. "I'm sorry," she said softly.

I held her gaze steadily for a few seconds. "Are you talking about Thomas and Charlotte? Or what happened between us before I left?"

"Both." She closed her eyes and shook her head. "More. Everything. I'm sorry for everything."

I let out a long breath. "These last two weeks would have been so much easier with you by my side."

"I know. I was foolish."

"About that." I poured myself a glass of wine to disguise the uncertainty in my face and tone. "Maybe you weren't so foolish."

Beside me, she'd grown completely still, a rabbit that knows the falcon is swooping overhead.

Be strong, Silas. Think of her life, not just of your own pitiful wants.

I took a deep breath. "When I saw you walk through the door tonight, I thought my greatest wish had been realized. That you had found me, and that I would finally be able to claim you in all the ways I wanted to—fuck you and marry you and spend the rest of my life loving you as your husband. But then I realized, as I was saying goodnight to the children, that this great wish wasn't actually my greatest wish."

"It wasn't?" she asked warily.

"No. You being happy is my greatest wish. And Molly, if you weren't sure you could be happy with me before..." Fuck, this was hard to say. Hard to do, knowing there was a good chance that she would take the escape I was offering. "I am the children's legal guardian now. And I love them. I plan on being as involved as their parents were, not only because they are dear to me, but because they deserve that, at least. That if they are going to be deprived of the two best parents the world has ever known, then at least I can try my hardest, even knowing that I'll fall short in so many ways."

Molly didn't speak, but her eyes searched my face imploringly, though imploring me for what, I didn't know.

"They mean everything, Molly," I continued. "So I guess what I'm trying to say is that they are bound to me. They are now, and forever will be, the biggest part of my life, and any woman who loved me would have to love them too."

I reached for her hand but she drew it away, her mouth growing tight. My stomach sank, but I finished my speech anyway, already steeling myself for the inevitable rejection. "I know the idea of an engagement scared you. And damn it all if the idea of being your husband isn't the thing I fall asleep dreaming about every fucking night—but I can't ask you to take on *this*. A family. Children you don't even know. And so, with all of my love and my blessing, I want you to know that I understand if you don't want to continue our relationship in whatever form it takes."

Her hands were balled in her lap and her mouth was set. "Do you really think I'm that heartless?" she asked in a low voice. "Do you really think I'm that cold? That I would have such distaste for recently orphaned children that I would rather not see you at all than get to know them?"

I sighed. "It would be more than *getting to know*, Molly. For all legal and emotional purposes, they are my children now. Traveling, working, even playing...everything has to change. It's a sacrifice that I make gladly, because I love them and because a big family is the vision I've always had for my own life, but I know that isn't what you've wanted for your-self. I can't ask you to give up your own vision and your own future."

"You don't think I apprehend that much?" Her voice had gone Irish in her anger, her words curling up into them-selves. Musical, lovely, and most of all, incendiary. "I'm not an imbecile, Silas, and I'm not some Jezebel incapable of warmth and compassion. I wouldn't abandon you simply because I didn't anticipate having a family in this way."

"But you're under no obligation to stay. To love me," I said gently. "This isn't your burden to bear. It's mine."

For a moment, I thought she was truly going to blow up and rain insults (and possibly physical blows) upon my head. But she turned away, staring straight ahead for a moment.

Then she stood up and walked over to my chair, kneeling in front of me.

My mind had no idea what was going on, but the moment her hands slid against the inside of my thighs, my cock leapt to happy attention, already half-hard just from her proximity alone. My body responded automatically in other ways—my legs spread to grant her better access and I trailed one finger down her neck. Goose bumps erupted across her skin.

"I want your burdens," she said. "I want to help you carry the weight of them. I want to..." her eyes blazed in the dark. "I want to *surrender* to you. I want you to exorcise your grief on me, I want you to use me to feel better. I want you to fuck me while you're angry, while you're furious and hurt."

"Even if I'm furious at you?"

"Especially then," she confirmed in a husky voice that went straight to my dick.

She laid her head against my thigh, looking up at me. "I was wrong. In London. I was scared and I didn't know what else to do, except stop everything from moving forward until I could figure out my own feelings. But when I got here, I realized that I didn't need to figure anything else out but this: I love you. I want you to own my heart, and the rest of me too."

Hope unfurled itself inside me, waving gentle tendrils of joy. But my voice remained distant and calm as I said, "You want me to own you?"

"Yes. And use me. Please." She lowered her gaze. "I'm submitting to you right now. Not because you've tricked me into it or forced me into it, but because this is how I want our lives to be. I want to be yours. Please say yes."

This was the first time she'd ever willingly and intentionally submitted to me, and the act was so incredibly erotic and also so poignantly sweet that I warred between kissing her and shoving the first ring I could find on her finger or wrapping my hand in her hair and fucking her mouth until I came all over those freckled cheeks and that insolent mouth.

I settled for something in between, because even though I wanted to do both of those things, I was also tired of being heartbroken over Molly O'Flaherty. I had to know she meant what she was saying.

"So you want me?" I asked her, a little sternly.

She nodded, eyes still down. Meek and demure. I liked this side of her, although I still wanted her fire and temper too. I would have both, I decided.

"Then you have to prove it."

"Prove it?" she echoed, nervousness and excitement both evident in her tone.

"Stand up."

With a questioning look at me, she obeyed. I stood as well and walked behind her, finding the buttons of her dress and slowly working them open.

"I never want you to change who you are outside in the world," I told her as the back of her dress fell open and I slid it off her shoulders. "I love you and respect you as that woman. But right here, right now, you are nothing more than my plaything, you understand?" The petticoats unlaced, I yanked the dress and the petticoats down to the ground, tossing them to the side once she'd timidly stepped out of them.

Now her corset, and she shivered as I pulled impatiently at the stays. "No thoughts," I said in her ear as I worked. "No doubts. No fears or worries. Your only responsibility right now is to please me and to remember your safe word if things get to be too much. Understood?"

I saw her shoulders straighten as she nodded, as if an invisible weight had been lifted. I loved that seeming contradiction between submission and freedom. And I knew that's what she needed, even if she couldn't articulate it.

A place to be safe and cared for. A place to be unconditionally worshipped. A place to be her nakedest, rawest self.

Corset and chemise divested, she stood in only her stockings and heeled boots. "Bend over and brace your hands on the arms of the chair."

With only the barest hesitation, she did as I asked.

"Worried someone will see you?" I asked as I unfastened my pants. I didn't bother to undress myself any further, simply freeing my cock and fisting it as Molly bent at the waist and spread her legs.

Shit. If there was a more gorgeous sight than this redhead bent over and presenting her pussy for me, then I didn't know what it was.

"I'm not worried," came her voice. "If you want me to be seen, then I will be. If you don't want me to be seen, then you'll make sure it doesn't happen. I trust you."

Those words dug into me in the best sort of way, and I closed my eyes, pressing the flat of my palm against her spine. "Good," I rasped. "It's good that you trust me."

Opening my eyes, I let go of my erection to cup her cunt. It was hot. So hot, and…

"So wet," I managed, my erection now a thing of needy, insistent stone. I was so hard it hurt, so hard for *her* and that tight cunt, and it had been so long. And it was *her fault* that it had been so long. Angry lust, bitter arousal, took hold of me. "Have you been wet all this time, Molly?"

"Since you took my hand in the courtyard. Please, Silas." She pressed back into my hand, seeking friction. "God, please touch me."

My hand cracked against one smooth ass cheek. "That's not how this works, buttercup. I use you, not the other way around. I'm so fucking angry with you right now, and I'm going to punish you until I'm satisfied you've learned your lesson."

I could tell by the way she shuddered and her cunt grew hotter and more swollen that this idea aroused her immensely. Of course, we both knew, deep down, that my growling orders and dark assertions were coupled with the certain knowledge that I would make sure she had just as much pleasure (if not more) than me. That was the topsy-turvy beauty of dominance and submission, something Castor and Julian had tried to explain to me several times but I'd never really understood.

Until now.

Until tonight, with the woman I loved panting and whimpering as I used both hands to spread her cheeks apart, exposing that glistening cunt and tight, pink asshole. I leaned over to give both several hot, messy open-mouthed kisses, and then I stood again, slapping her ass for good measure and smiling wickedly at the yelp she gave.

I placed the flared tip of my cock against her pussy and left it there, loving the way it looked as it slowly pressed inside. I reached over to the table and found a small silver ewer containing the oil meant to be eaten with the herbed bread I'd brought out for Molly's dinner. She gasped as I drizzled it down her ass and onto her pussy, making my shaft slippery and slick in the process.

And then I thrust home, driving her up onto her toes. I followed her, stepping closer and forcing her to bend down at an even steeper angle, fucking her mercilessly. "Does it hurt?" I asked her. "I want it to hurt. Like you fucking hurt me. I will break your body like you broke my heart."

She groaned at that, wriggling her ass back into me.

The oil made everything impossibly slick and slippery, and it took no effort to drag my thick cock out of her tight pussy and then ram it in again. Which I did repeatedly.

"Yeah," I grunted, wrapping one hand tightly around her

hip as the other stole down to the small pleated entrance that I really wanted. "That's so fucking good, Molly."

I pressed the pad of my finger against the firm, thin skin of her asshole and the oil made it so that it just slipped right inside. She gasped again, and I never stopped stroking myself with her pussy, I simply slid a second finger in her ass and then teased and prodded and thrust until her ashamed gasps gave way to something needier. More primal.

"I'm going to fuck your ass now, and you're going to come when I do. The servants might see." I reached for the ewer once again, slathering her ass and my dick in even more oil. "They might be watching right now, especially the men who stay at the edges of the property. They work the lavender fields. They're young men, strong men. Maybe I'll let them have a turn with you, hmm? Maybe we'll just leave you here covered in oil, and force you to come over and over again, on cock after cock, until you can't stand any more. Sluts do that, Molly. Would you like to be a good little slut tonight?"

"Oh God," she whispered, trembling. "Oh God."

I pulled out of her cunt and pulled my fingers out of her ass. And then my crown was right there, pressed against that spot that haunted my fucking dreams, and then she opened to me, oh so slowly, squeezing the head of my cock until I thought it couldn't possibly be squeezed any more, until I thought I would come that very instant, and then I was in.

"So fucking good," I muttered as my dick slowly disappeared between her cheeks. "Needed this. God, I needed this. Going to come so hard." It was so difficult to think coherently when my entire shaft was being clenched by her luscious ass.

"It's so big," she whimpered as I worked my way up to the hilt. "Hurts."

"It doesn't hurt me," I said, knowing it was cruel. But

despite my harsh words, I was already gentling her legs and her lower back right now, dropping one hand around to find her clit and rubbing it gently, so that her moans of discomfort slowly shifted into something more amorphous. The kind of discomfort that felt so strangely good that you didn't want it to stop.

And I wouldn't have a problem with never stopping. Her ass was the hottest, slickest fist, it was the tightest, dirtiest channel, and my balls were so tight and heavy with the need to come inside of her. I reached up and laced one hand into her hair, yanking her head sharply up and forcing her to arch her back and curve upwards. And my other hand found her nipples—hard little furls—and I pinched them each in turn.

"I fucking love your tits," I told her. "And your ass. I fucking love having you bent over and humiliated for me." She shuddered again and I knew she was seconds from coming. I dropped my hand and spanked her clit several times in rapid succession, and with something between a sob and a shriek, she came, her ass gripping me even tighter than before.

"Yeah, that's it," I muttered, looking down to watch my cock move in and out of her ass. "Make me come, Molly."

Her thigh muscles were seizing and fluttering against my legs and her hands were clenched around the chair and her cries echoed off the portico floor. And then she reached back and found my hand, squeezing it tight as a second orgasm chased her first, wracking her body and tugging hard on my cock like nothing I'd ever felt before.

But it was the clasped hands, like she needed me to anchor her pleasure, like she needed reassurance that I was here with her to keep her safe and loved while she fell over the edge—that's what clawed up from the base of my spine, an undeniable and primal need to mate, to fuck, to shove my cock deep in her ass and shoot hot jets of cum inside of her darkest, dirtiest place.

I fucked her as it ravaged up through my balls, fucking her so hard that she fell forward and I fell with her, mostly breaking her fall, but still sinking my cock deep into her ass as we both landed on the ground, her on her stomach and me on top.

"Here it comes," I growled. "That's it—*fuck*, that's it—"

I drove mercilessly down into her as the first pulse of seed shot inside, down and down and down and she was coming again, but all I felt was her tight entrance and the heat of my semen and the delicious, plump globes of her ass pressing against my groin as I fucked and fucked and fucked, like a brute that couldn't get enough.

It was impossible to get enough.

I finally, finally stilled, sweat dripping from my face, my body reeling from the aftershocks of the best climax I'd ever had. Braced up on my hands, I dipped my head low to hers. "I love you," I said quietly. "Are you okay?"

She tilted her face up to me and gave me a smile so rare and so sunny that I was instantly hard again. I flipped her over and started kissing her, fucking her ass once more—slowly and sweetly now—as I played with her clit and her pussy, and we were both once again lost to each other under the stars.

CHAPTER 12

SILAS

*T*hat night, there were baths and more fucking and more kissing and then more fucking again, and when I woke up late the next morning, my dick hurt in all the best ways. I rolled over to find Molly and bury my face in her cinnamon-scented neck, but she wasn't there.

Blinking and yawning, I sat up, for a moment entertaining the unfounded panic that she'd left abruptly last night after I'd fallen asleep, or that—worse—it had all been some sort of grief-induced hallucination.

But no. When my room finally came into view, I saw Molly in a fresh dress of ivory linen sitting at my desk, framed in a honey-gold square of autumn sunlight. Tears tracked down her face as she stared into her lap, and I was up out of bed in a second, my heart pounding with fear.

"Darling, what's wrong?" I asked, not stopping to pull on anything other than the loose unbuttoned trousers I'd fallen asleep in.

What if the warm light of day had exposed how fragile our promises of last night were? What if she was struggling for a way to tell me that she couldn't possibly stay with me?

She looked up, tears clinging to her long eyelashes. And that's when I saw my unfinished, unsent letter in her lap, turned to the last page.

My face burned with shame. "I never meant for you to see that," I mumbled, reaching for the papers.

She held them fast, tears continuing to fall. "Silas, you never told me…so many of the things in here…"

I burned even more, ashamed to have my unfiltered thoughts and feelings exposed with no warning, and also not a little frightened that she was angry with me. I said things in that letter that I would have never spoken out loud; it was a letter composed entirely out of my own need for catharsis, not a missive expounding sentimentally on my love. There were sections where I railed against her, sections where I railed against myself, long sections where I detailed precisely all the things I wanted to do to her body. Lust and anger and grief and wonder twisted together in its scribbled paragraphs, layers of emotion that even I—the author—wouldn't be able to precisely pick apart.

But Molly didn't stand up and slap me. She didn't demand to leave this instant. Instead, she rested her head against my hip, tears still streaming quietly down her face.

"I'm sorry," I said. "It was—I was never going to send it. But I had to write it."

Her hand slid around the back of my leg as she hugged my body closer. "I'm not angry, Silas. I'm sad that I hurt you and I'm sad that you hurt me, and most of all, I'm sad that you didn't say all of this to me last year."

I stroked her hair. "You're not angry with me?"

"No. Far from it. I'm amazed. You love me so much. I could feel it in every word of the letter, even the irate ones."

"I love you," I said. "I love that you're mine."

She nodded against my hip, nuzzling her face in the place where my thigh met my groin, and despite the marathon fucking of last night, despite the completely inappropriate context, my cock stirred to life, thickening and lengthening in my trousers.

I meant to say *sorry* again, but the word died on my lips as Molly rubbed her tear-stained cheek against my erection.

Shit.

That shouldn't turn me on. That was *wrong*.

But I knew by now that the man I was when I was with her was wrong in all senses of the word, and that fighting it was pointless.

"Take it out," I said.

She eagerly complied with my order, frantic hands parting the front of my pants and drawing out my cock, already full-hard. And then she did something that made my toes curl against the tiled floor of the villa: she reached one slim hand even deeper into my trousers and cupped my balls.

"Holy fuck," I whispered as she tugged my pants down farther and then started licking at my balls, sucking and nibbling and then pulling them into her mouth one at a time, the hot suction practically making my eyes roll back in my head. Her tongue swirled and darted, until she had worked her way to the base of my cock.

I dug my fingers into her hair. "Open up," I commanded hoarsely, and she did, parting her mouth and looking up at me with a look that was obedient and yet not at the same time.

The moment my crown touched her lips, I lost all semblance of control, holding her head as I roughly slid the rest of the way in, only stopping once I hit the back of her throat. As I drew my erection back out, she dragged the flat of her tongue against the sensitive underside, making me groan.

"*Fuck*, Molly. Just. *Fuck.*"

I pushed back in again, pushing a little farther this time and forcing her throat to open to me. I could feel her nose against my stomach, and it was possibly the most erotic thing I'd ever felt. I pulled out and then began fucking her mouth in earnest now, loving the feel of her plush lips and that naughty tongue, her involuntary noises, and yes, even loving the occasionally graze of her teeth.

"I love fucking your mouth, doll. You look so pretty like this. My pretty girl."

She moaned around me, and I lost it. I yanked her head back and fisted my cock, my hand flying hard and rough over my shaft.

"My. Pretty. Girl," I grunted, and then it came, the warm lashes of seed across her perfect face, and I grunted more obscenities though it all, thinking about her filthy mouth, about how I was going to make her suck my balls every morning right before I fucked her perfect little ass.

The thing about Molly was that even standing with my hand in her hair and my cock in my hand and her face covered with my seed, I still didn't feel sated. Not in the least.

Sending up a quiet prayer of thanks for Bertha and the servants for being around to care for the children, I scooped my woman into my arms and carried her to the bed, flipping her skirts up to her waist the moment I dropped her there and burying my face between those slender, freckled legs.

MOLLY

Six Weeks Later

For London, it was the best November day we could have hoped for. The sheets of cold rain had abated, leaving a high and clear sky. A little anemic and a little cold perhaps, but there was enough warmth here below to make up for it.

"I'm afraid I don't know much about hair," Ivy murmured, stepping back from me. She was already in her light blue attendant's dress, and across the hall, playing dolls in the library, Aurora and Jane were in their snowy muslins, ready to sprinkle a path down the church aisle with flower petals.

I turned and twisted in my seat to get a better glimpse of my hair. Despite Ivy's demurral, she'd done a beautiful job, the curls coiling and weaving in and out of a delicate up-do that exposed the lines of my neck and shoulders.

I stood and faced her. "Thank you."

She gave me one of her inscrutable dark-eyed looks, one of those looks that reminded me of a deer in a forest. "You're welcome."

I nodded. We were growing closer, Ivy and me, perhaps a natural consequence of loving two best friends. And, I had to admit, Ivy had been an invaluable resource when we'd returned to England last month and I'd found myself a new mother to five children. *And soon a sixth*, I thought to myself. But I didn't betray this thought outwardly; even Silas didn't know. I was saving the news as a wedding present. How funny that when he'd first come back to London, he'd asked me to give him a child, and now here we were, about to be married with one burrowed secretly inside my womb. It thrilled me and terrified me all at once, but so did most of the emotional frontiers Silas pulled me across.

Ivy surprised me by pulling me into a hug. Her arms slid

around the hollows of my waist, and she pressed herself against me. This was the most physical contact we'd had since that night more than a year ago at Markham Hall, where we'd stripped her naked on the floor of the parlor and introduced her to our version of Blindman's Bluff.

And then I flushed a little, because Ivy probably didn't know how frequently she and Julian figured into the fantasies Silas and I whispered to each other as we fucked. I stepped back, a little, my face feeling hot, and she regarded me with interest.

"Is everything okay?" she asked.

"Perfectly fine," I assured her. "Never better."

With my hair finished and my gown—a thing of pale gold with a draped silk skirt and a long train—securely buttoned, the cathedral veil was the last thing left. We pinned it to my hair, and then tasked Jane with carrying the back of it as we walked to the carriage, so that it wouldn't drag on the ground.

True to my word, I had indeed forced Silas into the papist faith. At least, forced in the sense that we paid a French priest a handsome sum of money to baptize Silas without the time and delay of his undergoing a formal catechism. And so it was to a Catholic church we went, exiting the carriage in a cloud of silk and lace and muslin.

The ceremony was nothing more than a blur. I remember seeing Ivy and Julian at the front, Julian's hand comfortingly on Silas's shoulder. I remember Jane and Aurora and their petals. I even remember the priest's sonorous baritone as he recited the ritual Latin that bound Silas and me together.

But mostly I remembered Silas, the stained glass painting his face with jeweled light, his eyes bright with happy tears as he affirmed his vows to me, and the way he bit his lip to keep from crying when I affirmed my vows to him.

I remembered the way his hands felt in mine, warm and

solid even through both pairs of our gloves, and the way his lips crashed against mine after he lifted my veil, firm and possessive and also curving into a smile against my mouth, because it was Silas and he was happy and so of course he was smiling.

And then there were the congratulations and the bells and the rice thrown, and then it was just me and Silas in the carriage, rolling back to his townhouse. The children would stay with Ivy and Julian and Bertha here in London while Silas and I went to Brighton for a handful of days for our honeymoon. Even Brighton would be dreary at this time of year, but I didn't plan on spending much time exploring the scenery.

"Come here, Mary Margaret," Silas commanded, patting his lap, and I made my way across the carriage to straddle him, piles of silk and tulle bunched around us. His gloved hands found my legs under all the fabric and swept up the length of my stockings. "My wife," he murmured, his hands wandering higher.

Only a thin layer of linen and the fabric of his trousers separated me from his quickly growing erection. I made a *mmm* noise in my chest, feeling how thick and how hard he was underneath me, feeling his hands finally grip my ass and lift me up. I pulled at his trousers as he ripped at my drawers, and then I felt the wide crest of his crown as it sought entrance, as I sank down and it slowly, deliciously, split me in two.

"My wife," he said again, wonderingly this time, as I took him all the way in. I started grinding down against him, silk rustling all around us, his gloved fingers still gripping my ass.

"I have something to tell you," I said, still working myself against him.

"Anything," he breathed, his eyes glazed and sex-bright. "Tell me anything."

"You remember the night of the engagement ball?"

"I only care to remember one part," he said, a little wary now.

"I'm talking about that part."

His mouth relaxed, even as he started thrusting up as much as his seated position would allow.

"There is something I've taken, since I was a girl. To prevent pregnancy." I watched his face for any sign of judgment or disapproval, but there was none. Relieved, I went on. "Well, I forgot to take it that morning. And every morning since I went to France."

His body stilled under mine, though those hands clung on to me even tighter.

"I...I wasn't certain last month. So I saw a physician last week, and he confirmed it for me. We think the probable conception date was that night." Another deep breath. "In seven months, we should have a child of our own."

The biggest smile I'd ever seen split his face, a wide and astonished grin, and then he was kissing me hard, his hands moving and finding my waist and then my hair and then my face, which he cradled in his hands as he broke our kiss.

His eyes searched mine. "Truly?"

"Truly." I brushed the back of my hand against his face, loving the faint rasp of the stubble against my glove, loving the sharp excesses of his features. With a finger, I traced a spiral around the dimple that drove me crazy. "We are going to have a child."

"God, I want to get you pregnant again just for saying that."

I giggled, which made me tighten around him, and he groaned, his smile shifting into something more feral, more determined.

"Why don't we give it a try anyway?" he said in my ear,

and within moments, we were both gasping through our first orgasms as man and wife.

I do rather think I could get used to being married.

EPILOGUE

SILAS

NINE MONTHS LATER

COUNTY CLARE, IRELAND

"I'm not an invalid, you know," Molly said snappishly, refusing my hand as we picked our way down the jagged path to the seashore.

I grinned up at her, loving her like this, fiery and unbound, her hair blowing free around her face, her eyes squinting ahead toward the sea. Surrounded by the rolling green above and the slate gray rocks below, she seemed so at home here, so natural. So content.

Except of course, when she didn't want me to help her.

"It's only been two months since the baby," I said. And then she stopped walking and planted her hands on her hips, looking dangerously close to launching into one of her rages, and I grinned even more because, *fuck*, she was so beautiful like this. Her hair more copper than scarlet in the bright sunlight, her eyes more summer sky than deep blue sea. Her Molly-ness wrapped around her like a selkie skin.

I put my own hands on my hips, pretending to toss my hair and glare just like her, and despite herself, she smiled.

"Fine. You can help me. But I'm not happy about it."

"I'll make it up to you later," I told her in *that* voice and she shivered.

When we got to the beach, we found a flat section of rock that was sun-warmed and more or less secluded from view and spread out our blankets. This was meant to be a picnic, but it was also a bit more—the doctor had cleared Molly for *resumption of marital affection* and I planned on taking my sweet time with that resumption and rewarding my brave woman for every minute of agony she'd endured to bring forth little Tamsin Charlotte into the world.

After our honeymoon, I'd surprised Molly with a trip to County Clare, where we'd purchased a cozy but comfortable house along the coast. Unfortunately, my duties with Coke Manor—which was now officially Albert's and that I ran as his manager until he came of age—and Molly's business kept us permanently anchored in England. But every chance we got, we made the trip to County Clare, and Molly had known the instant we'd purchased the house that she wanted to give birth here in Ireland. So we'd installed ourselves here a few months before Molly's expected due date, the children and Bertha and now a tutor and a governess.

Her pregnancy had gone smoothly, and though I would never say that the birth had also gone smoothly, knowing how much suffering went into it, both my wife and my daughter were healthy and alive at the end, a fact I thanked God for every day.

I loved my magical little Tamsin, her deep blue eyes

and bright red hair, her little face, her little chirps and sighs at night as she laid in her cradle next to our bed. I loved my strong, intelligent wife. Together, with my nieces and nephews, we made the best family a person could hope for.

I was the luckiest man alive.

"Lay back," I told Molly, and she wriggled back onto her elbows, regarding me with interest and a little trepidation.

That was okay. I was going to ease her back into things at her pace. If she wanted slow, I'd give her slow. If she wanted rough, well then, I'd be more than happy to give her rough. Honestly, after eight weeks, I would be happy just to last longer than a few minutes.

But first...

I settled myself between her legs, dragging the hem of her skirt up past her knees, past the line of her stockings, and up to her waist. I sucked in a breath when I saw that she had nothing else on—no drawers—and so her cunt was on full display for me.

"Fuck," I groaned, my cock already throbbing for her. *Start slow, start slow* my mind chanted. My cock had other ideas.

Ignoring it, I lowered my face and began kissing the sensitive skin of her inner thighs. I could smell her, and unable to resist, I dragged the tip of my tongue through her folds. "God, you taste so good," I mumbled into her thigh. "Want to fuck you so bad."

"I want you to fuck me too," she said. "But first I want you to lick me again. Please—*oh*. Yes. Like that."

I looked up at her as I swirled my tongue around her entrance and then sucked her clit into my mouth. Her eyes locked on to my own as her lips parted and she started panting fevered pleas *more* and *faster* and *make me come, please make me come*. And then she fell onto her back, squirming so hard that I had to clamp a forearm around her hips to hold her still.

It didn't take long, which I suppose is what you get after eight weeks of enforced celibacy. Within a few moments, her back was arching off the blanket and her cries were echoing throughout the cove and I was so hard that I couldn't think about anything else, except maybe also my wife's wet pussy in front of my face.

She pulled me up and over her, snaking a hand around my neck and moving my face down to hers, not so much kissing me as licking her taste from my mouth, and it took all of my self-control not to shove into her right then and there.

"Pull it out," she told me. "Put it inside me."

Well, I always aim to please.

I unbuttoned my pants and slowly fed inch after inch into her tender cunt, as she wrapped her legs around my waist and dug her heels into my back, pulling me closer, until I was completely sunk and our pelvises were flush together.

And together we rocked, slowly, gently, until she was urging me faster, urging me harder, and then her back arched underneath me again and I finally let go, pumping eight weeks worth of denial into her, pumping my cum deep and hot into her, and before I'd even completely finished, she was rolling us over so that she was sitting on top of me, holding up her skirt to expose the erotic sight of my cock buried inside of her.

"Make me come again," she begged, and the sea breeze played with her hair, sending long crimson strands blowing out behind her as she rode me. "Fuck, Silas, I love you so much."

"I love you so much, Mary Margaret. Now ride me harder. Make *me* come again."

She bit her lip, my words arousing her, and then she complied, my good girl. And both of us came, twice more, before I finally carried my bride back to our home and our family, where Tamsin greeted us by demanding to nurse for two hours and the children insisted I read *The History of Tom Thumb* in its entirety.

And the rest of the night passed with Molly by my side, a content Tamsin snuggled in her arms, and my nieces and nephews laying on the large rug by the fireplace while I read, all the while dazed by the fact that this was my life. *My life.*

My home.

My family.

My wife.

See? I told you I was the luckiest man alive.

Thank you so much for reading *The Wedding of Molly O'Flaherty*! I hope Silas and Molly's emotional (and kinky) road to their happily ever after was as fun for you to read as it was for me to write.

And if you like kinky, feels-y romance, you might want to check out *A Lesson in Thorns*, the first book in my sexy, gothic Thornchapel Quartet…

Keep reading to find out more!

WANT TO FIND OUT WHAT THE MARKHAMS ARE UP TO IN THE PRESENT DAY?

Have adventurous taste? Love all things kinky and dirty? Then try Proserpina Markham's story in *A Lesson in Thorns*, a tale of fateful romance and carnality set on the foggy English moors . . .

Twelve years ago my mother disappeared into the fog-shrouded moors of Thornchapel.

I left her memory there, along with the others. Of my

childhood friends, playing in the woods. Of the crumbling, magical world we found, and of the promises we made beneath the wild roses. I moved on, building a life as a librarian in America, far away from the remote manor where my mother was last seen alive.

And then the letter arrives.

A single word, in her handwriting, calling me back to England. Followed by a job offer I could never refuse, from a person I never could resist: Auden Guest. The new owner of Thornchapel, the seductive, elegant man I met as an imperious little boy when we were both children. Inside his private library, I begin to uncover the ancient secrets of the house--and the ones hidden inside my heart.

It's so very easy to be drawn back into the world of Auden's friends . . . and into the world of his worst enemy, St. Sebastian Martinez. The beautiful and brooding St. Sebastian is as irresistible as he ever was, and the three of us can't seem to unknot ourselves from each other. From the hasty promise we three made all those years ago.

As Thornchapel slowly tightens its coil of truths and lies around us, our reluctant threesome starts unravelling into filthy, holy pleasure and pain. Together we've awakened a fate that will either bloom like a rose . . . or destroy us all.

From the author of the *USA Today* bestselling New Camelot series comes an original contemporary fairy tale full of lantern-lit rituals, hungry desire, and obsessions that last for lifetimes...

Find more about A Lesson in Thorns here!

Hot Cop

The Markham Hall Series:

The Awakening of Ivy Leavold

The Education of Ivy Leavold

The Punishment of Ivy Leavold (now including the novella *The Reclaiming of Ivy Leavold*)

The London Lovers:

The Seduction of Molly O'Flaherty (now bundled with the novella *The Persuasion of Molly O'Flaherty*)

The Wedding of Molly O'Flaherty

ACKNOWLEDGMENTS

My women: Laurelin Paige, Kayti McGee, Melanie Harlow, Geneva Lee, and Tamara Mataya. Thank you to Tamara for your amazing edits, and Cait, my formatter (who I am sure never ever cries when she sees my name in her inbox.) To Linda, Sarah and Candi, who muffle the outside noise so I can huddle in my cave.

To my Dirty Laundry Girls and the Literary Gossip Girls. Your support is amazing. To all the other blogs that have been so kind to Sierra Simone—TRSOR, Natasha's A Book Junkie, Shh Mom's Reading, Maryse's Book Blog, Schmexy Girl Book Blog, True Story Book Blog, Fiction Fangirls, and so many others that I know I'm forgetting. THANK YOU!

ABOUT THE AUTHOR

Sierra Simone is a USA Today bestselling former librarian who spent too much time reading romance novels at the information desk. She lives with her husband and family in Kansas City.

Sign up for her newsletter to be notified of releases, books going on sale, events, and other news!

www.thesierrasimone.com
thesierrasimone@gmail.com